SHE CHASES SHADOWS

AN ARTEMIS BLYTHE MYSTERY THRILLER

GEORGIA WAGNER

CONTENTS

PROLOGUE

THE EARLY MORNING AIR in Veneto was thick with mist, cloaking the ancient cobblestone streets and obscuring the shapes of grand villas that lined them. The scent of espresso mingled with the fragrance of blooming wisteria as the sun struggled to pierce the veil of fog common to northern Italy.

Martha checked her watch again. 6:15 a.m. Right on time for her daily jog. A creature of habit, she found solace in the simple routines that structured her life. She laced up her worn sneakers, adjusted her faded tracksuit, and took a deep breath before stepping out of her front door and into the hazy morning.

"Buongiorno, Signora Lombardi," Martha greeted her elderly neighbor with a warm smile. Their morning exchanges had become a comforting ritual, even if they only ever discussed the weather or their garden's newest blooms.

1

"Buongiorno, cara," replied Signora Lombardi, returning the smile. "Be careful out there today. The fog is thicker than usual."

"Always am, Signora," Martha assured her, giving a little wave before jogging off down the street.

As she moved through the sleepy neighborhood, she moved onto the road that cut through the winding path lined by old trees. Ahead, mist swirled between the trunks, providing an eerie, isolated path through the morning dark.

Martha's ears perked up at the sound of something peculiar. It was a soft but persistent scraping noise, like that of a shovel digging through damp soil. She strained to make out the source, her curiosity piqued. A slight hesitation crept into her mind as she debated whether to investigate further or continue on her familiar route.

"Probably just someone tending to their garden," she muttered, attempting to dismiss her growing unease. But the nagging feeling persisted; the sound continued.

There was a graveyard nearby, wasn't there? Behind the old church?

She continued on the path, warily, peering through the trunks, her eyes straining in the mist.

As Martha approached the wooded lot from which the digging noises seemed to emanate, she felt her heartbeat quicken with every step. Her senses were on high alert, her ears straining for any hint of movement amid the heavy mist.

"Hello?" she called out tentatively, her voice barely above a whisper. "Is anyone there?"

The only response was her own voice, bouncing back through the fog. She hesitated, weighing the potential danger against her curiosity. Maybe she ought to turn back?

Her morning run was important . . . but that didn't mean she couldn't take another route. . .

But no . . . No, she was being silly.

Sounds in the fog weren't something to be scared of.

Taking a deep breath, Martha steeled herself and cautiously stepped over a fallen log, her eyes darting around nervously as she ventured deeper into the lot. The scraping sounds grew louder, more distinct, and she couldn't help but shudder at the eerie atmosphere the mist created around her.

The fog swirled around Martha like spectral wisps, a ghostly dance that seemed to mirror the turmoil churning within her chest.

She squinted through the mist, her breath catching as she glimpsed a shadowy figure darting away into the woods. Their hurried footsteps echoed ominously in the still air, indicating their desperation to escape.

"Hey, wait!" she shouted, adrenaline overcoming her fear. But the fleeing figure disappeared from sight, swallowed by the dense fog and looming trees.

Her heart pounded furiously in her chest as she approached the spot where the figure had been. The moist earth clung to her shoes as she stepped forward, her eyes widening with horror at what lay before her.

"God, no," she whispered, her voice barely audible.

A dead body lay half-buried in a shallow grave, its lifeless eyes staring up at her accusingly. The victim's skin was pallid, drained of color and warmth, the once-vibrant soul now extinguished. Martha couldn't help but shudder at the sight, bile rising in her throat as she fought the urge to look away.

It was then she noticed the golden pendant gleaming brightly against the corpse's bloodstained shirt. The intricate design held a sinister allure, drawing her attention despite the horror surrounding it.

She stared in horror at the dead man's features.

But then, recognition dawned.

She knew this man.

Dread welled within her. Someone had killed him.

Shit.

Her breath caught in her throat. She held back a shout as she turned on her heel and sprinted back toward town.

CHAPTER 1

THE SMALL APARTMENT IN Venice was a dimly lit, cramped space with peeling wallpaper and creaky wooden floors. It was the kind of place where one could easily blend into the shadows and disappear from prying eyes. The narrow windows were covered with dusty curtains that had seen better days, allowing only a sliver of light to enter the room, casting an eerie glow on the faces of its occupants.

Artemis Blythe sat hunched over a rickety table, her piercing gaze fixed on a chessboard, one hand absentmindedly brushing her coal black hair from her face. She wore no makeup, no piercings, and dressed plainly and simply—as if she wanted to be invisible. Her mind raced with strategies for the game and for their precarious situation—for a week, they'd been in Italy.

A week of nerve-racking waiting. Fake passports and identities took time.

Helen sat across from Artemis, moving the black pieces. She had a distracted look on her beautiful features, her curling brown hair pulled back with a red ribbon.

"Check," Helen murmured.

Artemis countered by blocking her king with a knight.

Helen didn't hesitate; she took the knight. A sacrifice of the queen. Artemis frowned, leaning forward.

She'd calculated this move already . . . but had she miscalculated?

Years of chess tournament experience hadn't prepared her for the challenge of facing her own sister.

Her brow beetled, and she focused on the board, trying to arrange the pieces in her mind.

But it was distracting playing in the cramped Venetian apartment.

For one, she didn't enjoy playing with her family as an audience. Not just her father but also her brother.

Tommy stood by the window, nervously peeking through the curtains, his hands trembling slightly. His fear was palpable, but he tried his best not to let it show. Every creak of the floorboards, every distant siren sent a shiver down his spine.

She sighed, shaking her head.

Tommy wore his usual leather jacket and motorcycle gloves. His hair was pulled back in a ponytail, and his mismatched eyes were the exact opposite of hers. One blue, the color of frost, the other hazel gold.

Otto, Artemis's father, leaned against the wall, his handsome, middle-aged face etched with concern. His curly blond hair framed a face that could have been taken straight from the screen of an old detective show. With a charming smile and crinkling eyes, he exuded an air of confidence and cunning that belied his current circumstances. Yet underneath it all, there was a certain loose morality that made him difficult to trust completely.

Forester, a tall and scarred man, paced the length of the room, his disheveled hair and clothing giving him the appearance of a wild man. A deep scar on his palm stood out like a brand, a constant reminder of the danger they faced. He moved soundlessly around the cramped space, his alertness betraying his cautious demeanor.

Tommy and Forester hadn't been getting along recently, and the two men were like caged animals cooped up against their wills.

Forester's right arm was in a sling, encased in a heavy cast.

Tension hung thick in the air, as heavy and oppressive as the damp Venetian morning pressing down on them from outside. The five people in the room were bound together by their shared desire to stay hidden, to remain unnoticed amid the twisting alleys and canals of the ancient city.

Tommy fidgeted, his fingers drumming a nervous rhythm on the edge of the table. His eyes darted around the room, settling briefly on each person before flicking away again. His fear permeated the air like a foul odor. He swallowed hard, his Adam's apple bobbing.

"Artemis, we can't stay here," he whispered urgently. "We're sitting ducks. They could find us at any moment."

Artemis glanced at him, her bangs falling across her face. She brushed them aside with an air of irritation and fixed him with a cool gaze. "And where do you propose we go, Tommy? We've been over this. There's nowhere else for us to hide."

"Can't we just . . . I don't know, split up or something? Anything's better than waiting around for them to catch us!" His voice wavered, a crack in the façade, revealing his desperation.

"Who are you worried about?" Helen said softly.

"Er, the feds!" he exclaimed.

But Helen and Artemis both shared a suspicious glance.

Neither of them completely believed their brother was on the level when it came to his claims about his fears.

Tommy had stayed in Seattle a few weeks ago but had changed his mind since.

He was running from something but had refused to reveal what pursued him to his siblings.

"Splitting up would only weaken our defenses," Forester replied curtly. "We have strength in numbers."

Helen sat silently across the table, listening, as her gentle disposition often warranted her to, her curls matted against her forehead. Though she appeared lost in thought, every word spoken reached her ears, and her fingers twitched with the urge to intervene.

A sudden knock on the door shattered the fragile calm they had managed to maintain.

Panic flared in Tommy's eyes, and he looked to Artemis for guidance.

She stared at the door, tense.

They weren't expecting company.

"Get down," she ordered, her voice soft. As they scrambled to conceal themselves behind the furniture, Helen stood, her face a mask of serenity.

A voice called through the door in Italian. Even Artemis knew enough to recognize the word. Police.

Shit.

She stood by the table, sharing a sharp look with Cameron.

Forester's hands bunched at his side, staring toward the door, his body subtly readying to spring into action.

For a moment, the room was bathed in anticipation.

"Chi è?" Helen called out in flawless Italian, her voice steady and confident.

"Polizia," came the gruff response.

"Un momento," Helen replied, glancing back toward Artemis for a nod of approval. Stepping forward, she opened the door to reveal two uniformed officers.

Artemis kept back. Her father had drifted out of sight into the hall.

"Buonasera, signora," one officer greeted her, his eyes flicking over her. "We heard a disturbance coming from this apartment. A neighbor said there was shouting this morning."

"Capisco," Helen replied smoothly, her natural charm shining through. "It was nothing. Just the television."

As Helen continued to converse with the officers, buying time and weaving a convincing story, Tommy's panicked breaths slowed. Artemis watched from her hiding spot, her mind racing as she assessed the situation.

A fine sheen of sweat glistened on Tommy's forehead, his hands trembling as he clutched the edge of the worn wooden table where he sat out of sight. The tension in the small apartment was a heavy cloud that seemed to weigh down every breath. Artemis took to her feet, moving slightly to the left, making sure she was completely out of view now; she stood by the window, her gaze fixed on the narrow canal below, the reflection of the water casting a shimmering pattern on the ceiling above.

Tommy sidled up to her, also keeping out of line of sight from the door.

The two of them waited patiently as Helen spoke with the officers.

"I don't know what noise it was, sir," Helen replied to a question Artemis hadn't heard.

The officers spoke a bit more but then turned as if to leave.

Artemis felt relief wash over her.

Of course, the argument the neighbors had likely heard had originated with Tommy and Forester.

The two of them had nearly come to blows.

The men were used to living lone wolf lives, and trapping them in confined quarters was stretching them to their limits.

A few seconds later, the door shut completely, and Helen slid the chain over the lock.

Tommy released a pent-up breath.

"Is it going to be like this everywhere we go?" Tommy's voice cracked, and he swallowed hard, trying to keep his fear at bay. "Always looking over our shoulders?"

"Tommy, we just need to stay vigilant," Artemis replied, her tone measured and steady, also keeping low. She turned away from the window, her eyes meeting his. "We've come this far, haven't we?"

"Vigilant? I can barely sleep at night," he muttered, rubbing his temples with a shaking hand.

Otto looked bored from where he stood in the hall. He was shuffling a deck of cards, his fingers deftly performing tricks that should have been mesmerizing but only served to underscore the heightened state of apprehension that hung over them all.

"What are you actually scared of, Tommy?" Artemis murmured, her eyes having left the chessboard to study her brother's features.

"W-what?"

"You heard me."

"Nothing!" he retorted.

She frowned at him. "You're shaking like a leaf, brother."

"Not," he replied, truncating his sentences like he so often did when he got uncomfortable.

Her brother jammed his gloved hands into his leather pockets, slouching and moving back to the window to overlook the Venetian waterways. It was a sight to behold, and Artemis had partially chosen this location for the beauty but also because Venice was known as a tourist city.

Strangers coming and going wasn't alarming to the locals. But Tommy's behavior was starting to raise suspicions, and Artemis couldn't ignore it any longer.

"Tommy, please," she said softly, placing a hand on his shoulder. "We're here for you, whatever it is. You don't have to face it alone."

He flinched at her touch but didn't move away.

"It's nothing," he repeated, his voice barely above a whisper. "Just . . . some guys I owed money to."

Artemis drew back in surprise. "What? How much?"

"Enough," he muttered, his gaze fixed on the water below.

"How much is enough?" she pressed, her voice firm.

He hesitated, then finally spoke. "Fifty grand."

"Fifty grand?!" she exclaimed. "Tommy, how did you get mixed up in something like that?"

"I got in over my head, okay?" he snapped, finally turning to face her. "It's not like I planned for this to happen."

Artemis sighed, running a hand through her hair. "We'll figure something out. But you have to tell us these things, Tommy. We can't help you if we don't know what's going on."

"I know," he said, his voice suddenly small. "I'm sorry. I just . . . I didn't want to put you guys in danger."

"We're in this together."

Tommy gave her a small smile, his shoulders slumping in relief. "Thanks."

Helen snorted in laughter.

Artemis glanced over, then back at her brother, and her eyes narrowed.

"You're lying, aren't you?"

With a wink and a smirk, Tommy turned away again.

"What's really got you bothered?" she snapped. "Do you *actually* owe someone money?"

"Hell no," he replied. "I'm smarter than that."

Artemis pinched her brow with a frustrated sigh. "Any chance we can just skip ahead to you telling us what all this is really about?"

"Is that a duck?" Tommy was looking out the window with the sort of practiced nonchalance that told Artemis all she needed to know. Whatever was bothering Tommy was Tommy's problem alone. He wouldn't share it until *he* was ready and not one second sooner.

Even if it put the rest of them at risk.

Outside, the sun was just beginning to peek over the horizon, casting a pink and orange hue over the city. The canals were alive with activity as gondolas glided by, people hurrying about their business. The morning fog still lingered in parts of Venice, giving an ethereal feel to streets lined with historic architecture and colorful murals that told stories of times long ago.

At least their temporary hiding place was beautiful.

Tommy was staring through the window when he suddenly went still.

"Shit," he whispered.

"What?" Artemis said sharply.

But he yanked away from the window as if he'd been scalded.

She leaned over, her breath fogging the glass as she stared into the streets below.

"Get back!" Tommy snapped, tugging at her shoulder.

But she ignored his insistent grasp. Instead, she peered toward a group of broad-shouldered men that seemed to have alarmed her brother. Three of them. All of them wearing black suits, golden jewelry, and slicked-back hair.

They were scowling as they marched over a pure white bridge with a canopy so slanted it looked like it was melting. As they glanced around, one of them checked his phone and muttered darkly. The other two were more intently scanning the area, their eyes hard and unforgiving.

He had a sort of hunched posture, and with his stony face and hunched back he almost looked like a gargoyle on an old gothic church.

Artemis felt her heart skip a beat as she watched them pass below her window—three thugs in black suits who exuded menace and danger.

"Who are they, Tommy?" she demanded. "Get back!" he snarled.

He leaned forward again, trying to pull at her.

But this time, his motion caught the attention of the men below. They glanced up, eyes widening.

"Shit," Tommy yelped.

Artemis barely had time to register the automatics appearing from under the thug's jackets before the window in front of her exploded in a hail of gunfire.

CHAPTER 2

As THE GUNSHOTS ERUPTED, shattering the peaceful Venetian streets, Artemis gasped and instinctively ducked for cover, shouting at the others to take cover as well.

Shards of glass flew through the air around her as she scrambled toward the door, crawling on all fours as the buzzing roar of the automatics reverberated off the walls of the building. Bullets ricocheted wildly around her, and she felt a sharp sting in her arm as one grazed her flesh.

"Get down! Down!" Forester was yelling as he pulled Helen and Otto to the ground, grimacing as his arm in a cast broke his own fall.

Tommy, meanwhile, dove behind a couch, which now was pockmarked with bullet holes on the upper portion. Tufts of cotton jutted out from the rips in the fabric, slowly drifting to the ground like snowflakes.

Artemis could hear the men shouting outside the window, their voices filled with anger and menace. From the floor, she felt her heart pounding in her chest, her breath coming in short gasps as she tried to control the panic rising within her.

She saw Tommy out of the corner of her eye, his face white with fear as he peeked over the edge of the couch.

"We have to get out of here," he hissed.

Artemis nodded, scanning the room for any kind of weapon they could use to defend themselves.

"Get them to the back room!" Artemis called to Forester. "Keep them safe!"

Cameron glanced at her and hesitated. The rugged, handsome ex-agent was clearly loathe to leave her side. But he spotted the panic in her gaze and gave a quick nod before grabbing the arms of Artemis's father and sister and dragging them toward the back of the room.

The gunfire had temporarily stalled and sirens could already be heard in the distance, along with the shouts of civilians on the waterways, speeding up on gondolas to escape.

Now, Artemis heard the shattering of glass from below. The men had breached the building. They'd reach the second floor in no time.

Forester was busy helping Helen into the backroom when Tommy lurched to his feet.

He took two running steps and shoved Cameron into the room. Then, Tommy slammed the door shut as Forester yelled in anger.

He dragged the couch across the door, blocking it.

"What the hell are you doing?!" Cameron shouted, his fist banging on the inside of the door.

The ex-fighter's fist sent reverberating waves through the wood and through the room.

Artemis just stared in horror.

"Keep quiet!" Tommy whispered fiercely. "They haven't seen you yet. Just me and Artemis. Shut up!"

"I'm going to rip the leather off your soul!" Forester shouted back.

The door rattled, and though it was sturdy oak, it looked like it might splinter. The handle jiggled where it lodged over the dense couch cushions. Forester was still trying to get out.

But Tommy kept desperately speaking. "Look, you neanderthal—keep my sister safe! They didn't see her. Just the two of us."

"They're here for you, aren't they?" Artemis whispered.

Tommy glanced at her, frantic, guilt in his eyes. "There's no time!" he said.

She grabbed his wrist, squeezing hard. "Are they here for you?" "Y-yes. Just . . ."

"Forester, please," Artemis said quickly. "Stay quiet. Stay low. They didn't see you. Please, I'm begging you. Protect my family."

It was hard for her to say those words, especially given how much she wanted to slap Tommy.

But he was right.

For now, Otto and Helen were safe with Forester.

Cameron was safe.

The same couldn't be said for the two of them.

The front door to the apartment suddenly shivered, bits of wood scattering across the room as gunfire blasted the panel from the other side.

"Stay quiet," she said a final time, pleading.

And then she bolted toward the window, Tommy at her side.

Harsh voices shouted from the hall. More gunfire. Something zipped past her ear, but Artemis reached the already shattered window that overlooked the water.

She hesitated, only briefly, shooting a quick glance over her shoulder as Tommy came stumbling after her.

"Shit, Tommy," was all she managed.

The door clapped in its frame as a heavy boot threatened to batter the bullet-peppered door off its hinges.

Artemis's strategic mind didn't stop with chess. The facts of her situation flew behind her eyes as clearly as visualizing moves on a game board, and in a split second, she analyzed a dozen lines of attack and defense.

The shooters hadn't yet seen her family. They had to see her and Tommy leaving.

They had to be in a rush.

And so she waited until the very last second.

Wood cracked and hinges pinged as the apartment door was kicked in.

The men in the doorway swarmed in, shouting, guns raised.

And then, with a gasp, she leaped, yanking Tommy along behind her.

The two of them arched through the air together, plummeting toward the Venetian canal. Artemis's stomach dropped as her suddenly nerveless fingers lost track of her brother.

The icy water smacked her with a force that stole her breath away, her body sinking down, down, down into the murky depths. She felt her clothes dragging her down, and for a moment, she panicked, thrashing and flailing in the water.

But then she kicked off the silty floor, propelling back toward the light shimmering above.

She broke through the surface, gasping for air, the cold water shocking her senses.

She looked around, her heart pounding in her chest. She couldn't see Tommy.

"Tommy!" she screamed, her voice bouncing off the walls of the nearby buildings. "Tommy, where are you?"

There was no answer.

Artemis swam toward the nearest canal wall, her fingers scrabbling for purchase. She pulled herself up, her body shivering with cold, and looked around frantically.

There, on the opposite side of the canal, was Tommy, clinging to the wall, his body shivering with cold.

Artemis didn't hesitate. She plunged back into the icy water, swimming toward her brother. He was dragging himself from the murk.

"Watch out!" he shouted.

She glanced back and spotted the three men barreling out the front door, into the street. A part of her felt a grim sense of satisfaction; the approaching men hadn't noticed her family, her boyfriend.

The others were safe.

But Artemis and Tommy were sitting ducks.

A small motorboat was coming by, and Tommy had already spotted it, shouting as he swam toward it. The man in the boat frowned, trying to push Tommy away with his foot. But Artemis's brother grabbed the man's leg and dragged him into the water.

Artemis felt herself starting to protest, but what else could they do? She followed her brother's lead, clambering into the boat as well. More gunshots resounded now. Wooden chips erupted from the side of the white-painted boat.

Tommy was already maneuvering the vessel away from their building.

The three men were howling, sprinting across the same bridge they'd come over, trying to track them along the shore.

"They've got a boat!" Artemis warned.

Indeed, one of the men had commandeered another vessel. This one looked sleeker, faster . . .

She stared in horror as the canal zipped by beneath them and their boat sped rapidly forward.

One of their pursuers had a stony face and a hunched posture. He looked like the leader of the group and had taken the helm of the pursuing vessel.

Tommy was growing nervous as the other boat drew closer. "We've got to lose them," he muttered, his eyes scanning the water ahead.

Artemis could sense the tension in his body as he gripped the wheel, his knuckles turning white. She knew he was an experienced driver, but he preferred motorcycles on dusty roads to dilapidated speedboats on waterways.

The boat was gaining on them, its engine roaring louder with every passing second.

"They're gaining on us. We have to do something," she said urgently.

Tommy nodded, his eyes narrowing in concentration. "Hold on tight," he said, before yanking the wheel to the left.

Their boat lurched sideways, nearly tipping over as it skimmed across the water. Artemis gripped the sides of the boat, her heart hammering in her chest as they careened toward the canal wall.

"Jump!" he yelled.

The two of them leaped right before impact. The boat crashed into the wall and they both tumbled into the street, rolling to a halt.

But more gunfire quickly prompted them back to their feet. Venetians and tourists who initially froze and gawked at the crash now screamed and fled down every adjacent street and alley.

The men behind them continued shouting. Artemis could only hope Forester and the others had gotten to safety.

Now, with Tommy at her side, the two of them sprinted down another of the white stone bridges, racing away from the gunmen. Both were panting as they weaved through Venetian streets. Sirens wailed. Voices shouted.

The peaceful neighborhood was now one giant mess.

Artemis and her brother veered down one of the cramped streets Venice was famous for, the buildings towering above them. Artemis could feel the walls closing in on her as she ran, feeling more and more like a rabbit being chased into a snare.

The other speedboat had reached the shore too. She could now hear the gunmen's footsteps pounding behind them, growing closer with every passing second.

"Tommy, we have to find somewhere to hide," she gasped, her voice barely above a whisper.

He nodded, his eyes scanning the alleyways around them. "Keep moving," he said, his voice low.

He pulled at her arm, dragging her into a darker alley, barely a slit in the wall. The two of them had to turn sideways just to fit. Artemis and her brother both went still. She held her breath, listening. Her vision swam as her air-starved lungs instinctively tried to gasp for air, but she knew the sound would be too dangerous. She needed to take slow, *silent* breaths.

Shadows fell across the mouth of the alley.

The gunmen had arrived.

They walked slowly, their boots crunching against the cobblestones. Artemis could feel Tommy tense beside her, her heart hammering in her chest.

One of the gunmen looked sleeker and faster than the others, his body taut like a coiled spring. He had a gun strapped to his back and a knife in his belt. But it was the man with the stony face that sent shivers up her spine. He paused at the entrance to the alleyway, looking around suspiciously as if he sensed something was amiss.

She held her breath, standing in the dark and willing him to leave.

The gunmen glanced down a street across from them. Then another. The man with the hunched back stepped toward the alley where they hid.

But just then, there was a distant sound like a loud crash. The men jolted, turning sharply. A second later, there was the sound of an approaching siren. The men grumbled darkly to each other and then turned, hastening away.

Artemis didn't release her pent-up breath until the men were out of sight, but she let out a sigh of relief as she felt Tommy relax by her side.

"Phew," he whispered.

"Don't phew me," she said sharply, turning toward her brother, glowering. "Who are they?"

"Wh-what?"

"I heard them speaking, Tommy. Those aren't Italians. They had an American accent. Who," she said, jabbing him in the chest with an extended finger, "are they?"

He winced, trying to step back in the tight alley, but he was wider than her and the walls pincered him, holding him like a cork in a bottle.

"Shit, hang on! Fine. Fine," he said, whispering. "Not here . . . Just . . . Come. I'll tell you everything."

"No, Tommy! You're dodging."

"No, I swear. I'll tell you."

She glared at him, but slowly, she emerged from the alley, both of them glancing left and right, looking for any sign of their pursuers. But they were alone.

"Think that crash was your boyfriend?"

"Probably," Artemis whispered.

She felt a lancing pang at the thought of Cameron being left behind.

She bit the corner of her lip and moved slowly through the shade that filtered through the alleys lining the canals.

"So start talking," she said, looking at her brother. "Why are Americans hunting you in Venice?"

He winced, shooting her a sidelong glance.

"Fine . . . but you're not going to like it."

CHAPTER 3

THE CRISP AUTUMN AIR nipped at Artemis's cheeks as she and her brother sat at a small wrought iron table outside a quaint café. It was nestled in an unassuming corner of the town, miles away from the shoot-out location. The café was perched right on the water, giving them easy access to an escape route if needed.

Artemis's eyes kept scanning passersby, searching for the three gunmen. The audacity to open fire in a foreign city only made her more nervous. Whoever they were, they thought they operated above the law . . . that is, if they gave a rip about the law at all.

She absently twisted a lock of her dark hair around her finger, her features marred with worry. Despite her plain and simple attire, Artemis felt like she stood out amongst the colorful churn of locals and tourists.

"Can you hear them?" Tommy whispered, his eyes darting nervously around the square.

Artemis tilted her head slightly, picking up on the distant wail of sirens so faint that they nearly blended in with the background hum of the city.

"Still too close for comfort," she murmured, her sharp gaze scanning their surroundings.

"Maybe we should've gone farther," Tommy suggested, fidgeting in his seat.

"Let's just lay low for now," Artemis replied, her voice steady despite the chaotic thoughts racing through her mind. A chess master like herself thrived on anticipating her opponents' moves, but this situation had spiraled beyond her control.

She glanced at her waterlogged phone. She'd waited as long as she could before trying to boot it up. Waterproof—or so the device advertised.

And now, she was testing this theory. She felt a flicker of excitement when she spotted the new text notification.

"Are they alright?" Tommy said quickly, leaning in to see the phone.

She read a text from Forester. We're out. Safe. You?

She replied quickly. Fine.

Where? The answer came almost immediately, suggesting Cameron was glued to his screen, desperate for any news.

She hesitated and looked around then replied, Going to have to wait. Have to handle things with Tommy first.

Be safe.

You too.

She stared at the message chain, feeling a lump forming in her throat.

Artemis took a deep breath and closed her eyes, trying to calm her racing heart. She knew that she had to stay focused, that she couldn't afford to let her emotions get the best of her. She had to keep her wits about her if she wanted to survive.

She opened her eyes and looked at Tommy, who was nervously tapping his foot on the pavement. She placed a hand on his arm, feeling the tension in his muscles.

"Listen, Tommy," she said, her voice firm but calming. "We need to talk. No more stalling."

But just then they were distracted by an approaching waiter, balancing a tray of steaming food as he artfully retrieved their drinks.

"Two coffees," the waiter announced, placing steaming cups before them.

"Thanks," Tommy muttered, reaching for his cup with trembling hands. The waiter gave a bright smile and retreated, carrying the food to a nearby table.

Artemis eyed him warily before taking a sip of her own coffee, letting the bitterness ground her. For a brief moment, it helped her focus on the present rather than the dangers lurking around every corner.

The damp chill clung to Artemis and Tommy, their clothes still heavy with water from their recent swim. She could only assume the lack of comment from the café waiter implied they were not the first Americans he'd seen soaking wet from a fall into the canals. The discomfort was undeniable, but it served as a constant reminder of their need to lay low. Every shiver that ran down Artemis's spine was tempered by the knowledge that they'd escaped from something far worse.

"Here," Tommy said, thrusting a sweater in her direction. "I got this for you."

"Wh-what? Where'd you get that?"

She hadn't even noticed him carrying the thing when they'd sat. Her brother had a habit of picking up items that didn't belong to him.

She eyed him disapprovingly, refusing to accept the stolen garment. "I won't wear that."

"Suit yourself," he muttered, tugging on the pilfered sweater himself and suppressing a shudder.

She gave her brother a moment of silence to come clean, to tell her what he knew. Instead, he took another sip of his coffee. Artemis released a sigh through her nose. "Tommy, what's going on?"

"Uh, three guys with machine guns chased us into the canal. Come on, Art, you're supposed to be the observant one."

"Enough," Artemis said, her voice serious. "Tell me what's going on."

For a moment, she thought he'd continue to dodge, but Tommy's rapscallion smirk faded. He swallowed hard, his hands trembling in his lap. "Back in Seattle, I . . . I accidentally killed a mobster's son."

Artemis felt as though the air had been sucked from her lungs. Her heart thundered in her chest, and she gazed at her brother, disbelief clouding her eyes. The sound of the sirens seemed to grow louder in her ears, an ominous chorus that underscored Tommy's confession.

"Tommy, what . . . how?" she stammered, her mind racing with images of bloodshed and violence.

"I didn't mean to, Artemis," he said, tears welling in his eyes. "We were robbing a place, and I was just supposed to be the getaway driver. But things went wrong . . . I . . . we got in a chase. He started shooting at cops. I spun out and . . . I protected my side—it was instinct. He was crushed by a concrete barrier."

"How'd you get away?"

"Just ran. We'd distanced enough the cops didn't see us under the bridge at first. But they found him."

He swallowed and winced.

The weight of his words threatened to crush her, and Artemis clenched her fists beneath the table, her nails digging into her palms. Here they were, evidently on the run from the very people who sought vengeance for that terrible mistake.

"Tommy . . ." she breathed, struggling to reconcile the image of her brother with that of a killer. "Why didn't you tell me sooner?"

Tommy shrugged. "I mean, I kinda hoped being an international fugitive with the rest of you might let me lay low. You know, disappear until the heat drops." Scratching at his scalp, Tommy gave a mirthless chuckle. "I knew I should have just stayed away . . . There's a huge bounty on my head, and every heavy hitter in the country is probably booking flights to come after us now."

Artemis's pulse quickened at the thought of the danger they faced. She took a deep breath, attempting to steady her nerves and process the shocking revelation. She knew that, as a strategist, she had to remain calm and collected in order to find a way out of this dire situation.

"Tell me more about what happened," she said quietly, her voice steady despite the turmoil building within her. "I need to know everything to understand how best to handle it."

Tommy glanced around nervously, ensuring no one was paying them any undue attention. He leaned in closer, his voice nearly inaudible above the chatter of the café patrons.

"Alright," he began, hesitating momentarily before continuing. "It was supposed to be a simple job—just a small-time robbery at a local store. I was the getaway driver. We didn't expect anyone to get hurt."

He paused, swallowing hard. "But things went wrong. The owner's son . . . He came out of nowhere, trying to stop us. It wasn't intentional, but during the struggle, he ended up getting shot. I panicked, got everyone out of there as fast as I could, but the damage was done."

Artemis closed her eyes for a moment, allowing herself to fully absorb the weight of her brother's words.

"Did you . . ."

"No. Hell no. I didn't shoot him, Art. I swear."

Despite her natural inclination for logic and reason, she couldn't help but feel a pang of despair at the thought of her brother being involved in such a tragedy.

Tommy sighed, running a hand through his damp hair.

"Look, I didn't mean for any of this to happen," he continued, staring down at the table between them, his fingers drumming an anxious rhythm. "But when everything went sideways . . . I panicked. And I made a mistake that cost me everything."

She hesitated only briefly, then she slapped him across the face.

She hadn't meant to. In fact, she hadn't even known what she was going to do until her hand was already mid-motion. But as he hung his head, sounding sorry for himself, a flicker of rage prompted her hand.

He stared at her, more stunned than hurt.

"This isn't just about you!" she said sharply. "You almost got your family killed. My boyfriend!"

"Boyfriend," he snorted. "Three gunmen show up to kill your little brother and you're worried about that asshole?"

"No, Tommy—" she snapped. "You're the asshole. No, stop—I'm not finished. Shut up."

He closed his mouth again. She scowled at him.

"You need to listen to me, Tommy," she said, her voice low and fierce. "We're in this together, and we're going to get through it together. But you need to stop feeling sorry for yourself and start thinking about how we're going to survive."

Tommy looked up at her, his eyes wide and vulnerable. Artemis felt a pang of sympathy for him, but she quickly pushed it aside.

"Who's hunting you?"

"W-what?"

"Who's got the hit out? Is it someone who'd take a bribe?"

He stared at her. "No . . . well, not the type of bribe I could offer."

She shook her head, leaning back. She didn't mention to her brother how much money they'd earned on their last job.

More than a hundred million now sat in a bank account only she had access to. A gift from a billionaire's daughter. They had the funds. And mobsters were often loyal to only one thing above family.

"How can I speak with him?"

"W-who?"

"The father of the mobster that died."

"Shit . . . you can't just speak with him."

"Why not?"

"Because!"

"He'll try and kill me? He already did, Tommy."

He stared at her, flustered. "I . . . I mean . . ."

"Do you have a way of getting in contact with him?" she demanded.

He stared, hesitated, then ran a gloved hand through his pony-tail. "I mean . . . yeah. I guess." He trailed off, frowning at her.

"Good," she said, her tone firm and unwavering. "Then get me a meeting."

She pushed away from the table, her clothing still damp, the sound of sirens still drifting in the distance as she led her brother back into the Venetian alleys.

Artemis stared at the phone in her hand as if it were a ticking time bomb, her black hair obscuring her face as the Adriatic breeze tugged at the locks. Her thumb hovered over the call button, poised to connect her with Mr. Luciano. She knew that this conversation would be anything but pleasant, and she steeled herself for the confrontation ahead.

The two of them stood in the middle of a bustling tourist section of Venice, where the bright sun was drying their clothes. The air was thick with the smell of salt water and fresh seafood, while colorful umbrellas and flags lined the canals.

"Tommy," she said firmly, her voice devoid of emotion. "Stay close, but not too close. I need you to hear what's being said, but I don't want Luciano to know you're listening."

Her brother nodded once, his lips sealed as he stepped aside to lean against a white stone bridge arching over the Venetian canal.

"Understood," Tommy whispered, positioning himself by a marble column.

With a deep breath, Artemis pressed the call button and raised the phone to her ear. As soon as the first ring sounded she felt her heart racing in her chest, but her face remained expressionless.

"Luciano speaking," came the gruff voice on the other end, thick with impatience.

"Mr. Luciano," Artemis responded coolly, her tone measured and precise. "This is Artemis Blythe—Tommy said you were expecting my call?"

A grunt. She'd never heard such clear hostility communicated in a grunt before, but the man managed it all the same.

She swallowed. "We need to talk about the situation with Tommy."

"Ah, yes," Luciano sneered, anger boiling beneath the surface of his words. "The man who killed my nephew."

Artemis clenched her free hand into a fist, her nails digging into her palm as she fought to maintain control of the conversation. She had to make him see reason, convince him that Tommy was not responsible for his nephew's death.

"Mr. Luciano, I understand your pain, but I assure you Tommy did not kill your nephew," she stated, her voice steady despite the tension crackling through the line. "You need to hear us out and consider the possibility that you've been misled."

"Misled?" Luciano roared, his anger erupting like molten lava. "You think I don't know what I'm talking about? You think I don't have proof?"

"Sir, it was an accident."

"Bullshit. Tommy killed my nephew, and so his life is mine. Lucky piece of shit is getting kids gloves. Normally, I'd want him back alive."

Tommy, who was standing by the pillar, winced and tugged at his ponytail resting against his leather jacket.

There was a pause on the other end of the line, the silence heavy with unspoken tension and the weight of the past bearing down on them all.

"Alright," Artemis said, her voice unwavering. "I have a proposition for you." She glanced at Tommy, who was watching her with an unreadable expression.

"Who the hell are you to begin with?"

She blinked. "Tommy's sister."

A snort. "That right, Tommy?" he said, louder now, his voice distorting through the speaker. "You got your sister doing your chatting for you? Bitch."

She wasn't sure who this last word was directed at. She ignored it all the same.

"Why don't we get down to brass tacks," she said quietly. "I am willing to offer you a significant amount of money, enough to make it worth your while, in exchange for leaving Tommy alone."

"Money?" Luciano scoffed on the other end of the line. "You think you can buy me off like some common thug?"

"Of course not, Mr. Luciano," Artemis replied, careful to keep any trace of offense out of her tone. "This isn't a bribe. It's the blood price. If you come after Tommy, our family comes after you. I know you don't know me, but trust me when I say *much* more blood will be spilled before this is over."

Artemis shivered, trying to keep her voice calculated and confident, but despite meaning the words as a bluff, she couldn't help but remember the horrors her sister Helen, the *real* Ghost Killer, had been responsible for. It wasn't outside the realm of possibility that Tommy's assassination could unleash that monstrous side of her sister against these mobsters. "I know you want revenge. But this is better for everyone. Your nephew's blood has a price, and I'm willing to meet yours if it means keeping Tommy safe."

Not everyone had a price, but Artemis did believe that everyone in Luciano's line of work had one. There was a pause as Luciano considered her offer. Artemis's mind raced, trying to anticipate his response, calculating the risks involved.

"How much we talking?" Luciano said.

"A million," she replied coolly.

Tommy's eyes bugged from where he stood, staring at her. He opened his mouth as if to say something, but she held up a finger to hold back any words.

"A million? US?"

"Of course."

A snort. "You got that kind of cash?"

"Yes."

"Not wasting my time, are you, Artemis Blythe?"

A long pause. He was considering the offer—this was a good sign.

"Two million," he countered finally.

"Deal," she said without hesitation.

A sharp exhalation on the phone. "That easy, huh? You care for this brother of yours?"

"I guess," she replied, releasing a tired sigh. "So we have a deal?"

A long pause stretched, and Artemis looked down to be sure the call hadn't disconnected.

Finally breaking the silence, Luciano said, "Let's discuss this further, but not over the phone."

Artemis's heart leaped into her throat, her thoughts turning to all the ways such a meeting could go wrong. A trap, an ambush, a double cross—there were countless possibilities, each more dangerous than the last.

She forced herself to sound calm and collected. "When and where?"

"Two hours," Luciano replied, his voice dripping with menace. "I'll send you the location later. Just you and Tommy—no one else."

Artemis hesitated, her fingers tightening around the phone as she weighed the risks of meeting Luciano in person. She glanced at Tommy, his face pale and drawn with tension. Her heart ached as she considered the danger she might be putting him in.

"Mr. Luciano," Artemis began, her voice steady despite the knot in her stomach, "You must understand—we're willing to cooperate, but I need some assurances that Tommy will be safe."

"Assurances?" Luciano scoffed, his voice dripping with contempt. "You're not in a position to make demands, girl."

"Neither are you, Mr. Luciano," Artemis shot back, her eyes narrowing. "If you want this money—and I know you do—then we need to meet on neutral ground."

There was a moment of silence as if Luciano was weighing his options. Artemis's mind raced through possible meeting locations, each more crowded and public than the last. The more people around, the less likely Luciano would try anything dangerous.

"Very well," Luciano finally conceded, his tone grudging. "Where did you have in mind?"

"Campo San Polo," Artemis suggested, her voice firm. "At noon, near the statue of Paolo Sarpi. It's busy enough that we won't attract attention but open enough that we can see anyone approaching."

"Fine," Luciano growled, clearly displeased with her choice. "But remember, just you and Tommy."

"Agreed," Artemis replied, already planning their escape routes and contingencies. "We'll be there."

"Alright," Luciano said finally, his voice laced with reluctant acceptance. "Cash—and a favor."

"Hang on, what favor?" she said. "I didn't agree to any favor."

"You want your brother's life?" snapped Luciano. "My brother's son is dead. He wants Tommy's head. If I'm going to convince him to call off the hit, I'm going to have to sweeten the deal. Understand?"

"What favor?" she repeated more firmly. Her hand reached out, braced against the side of the marble bridge.

Below, she spotted a couple of gondolas slicing through the water. Tourists were tossing small bits of bread to birds flitting over the water.

She stared, wondering if she was being baited.

Of course she was.

She already had in mind to change the location last minute. She had the perfect location in mind. She'd seen it on their walk through the city streets.

But now, she felt her breath caught in her throat. She let out a faint, leaking exhalation, trying to calm her frayed nerves.

"We've had some trouble with our contacts over there," he said. "In Italy, I mean."

Artemis didn't reply yet, her eyes imperceptibly narrowing.

"Yeah," he said, answering his own question. "We've had trouble, and there's something Tommy can do about it."

Artemis didn't like the sound of this.

A few tourists were moving up the bridge now, glancing in her direction. She gave polite, curt nods, hoping they'd keep on walking, but they ended up leaning against the rail on each side of her, taking pictures of the skyline.

She sighed and moved off toward the pillar where Tommy remained. He opened his mouth to speak, but she held a firm finger over her lips, and he fell silent.

"Why not just tell me the favor now?" she said. "We can get this over with?"

"Nah. In person," he replied. "Cash. So we know there's no bullshit."

She sighed. "Fine. In two hours."

"Make it half an hour," he said. "And just you two. Alone."

He hung up, leaving Artemis with a pit in her stomach.

CHAPTER 4

ARTEMIS AND TOMMY ARRIVED at the five-star hotel they'd changed the meeting to. Luciano seemed to almost expect the move, and it was cold comfort to Artemis that he didn't object. Maybe the mobster wasn't plotting an ambush after all?

"You stay here," she said to her brother, frowning at him. "Don't show yourself." He glared at her. "I'm not letting you go alone, sis."

"Why?" she said. "Because it'd endanger me? You've already done that, Tommy."

She hadn't meant to be harsh, just factual. But she could tell by his grimace that her words stung. Still, there was too much going on to focus on any one thing.

She gave her brother a quick pat on the shoulder where they stood in the parking lot, and then she hastened toward the black gate leading to the swimming pool.

She'd wanted to meet at the pool, and she'd required a certain type of outfit.

And now, as she peered through the fence, she spotted the three thugs all standing there by the snack shack. Each of them was wearing a swimsuit.

No shirts. No shoes. The swimsuits were tight, giving very little room to conceal anything. No weapons.

She glanced around, making sure the coast was clear, her gaze taking in every scene. Her mind cataloged information rapidly, searching for potential threats.

The pool was large, and the crystal-clear water glistened in the bright sun. The air was humid, and a light breeze had begun to pick up, ruffling her hair. The aquamarine tiles were cool against her feet as she stepped onto them, their speckled pattern leading her toward the edge of the pool.

The sound of laughter echoed throughout as people chatted with one another or just enjoyed a peaceful moment by themselves enjoying nature's beauty. The three men by the shack, though, weren't smiling at all. The one with the gargoyle glower glared at her, his rigid features fixating as she approached. Either he had lockjaw or a significant amount of plastic surgery. She couldn't tell if the plain-faced man was fifty or twenty-five.

She hesitated as she drew near, watching them, pausing only briefly to check over her shoulder to make sure Tommy hadn't been dumb enough to follow her in.

She paused, meeting the gaze of the gunmen. None of them carried weapons currently.

She swallowed briefly.

She wasn't sure when she'd become her family's caretaker, but she was beginning to resent the role provided to her.

She let out a faint sigh, rubbing the edges of her eyes before approaching the three men by the snack shack, nodding to each of them in turn.

The one with the hunched form stepped forward. "Blythe?" he said, his voice rasping.

She nodded. "And your name?"

He didn't reply. He simply said, "Cash?"

"Nearby," she said. "I wanted to talk first."

He frowned at her. "No cash, no deal."

"I have the cash," she retorted. "It's nearby."

There was a loud splash as a child flung himself off the high dive, and small flecks of water speckled her pale skin.

She reached up, flicking the droplets away, and the three men tensed. The one on the left moved his hand toward his pocket. A concealed weapon?

She shifted uneasily. At least for the moment, she wasn't dead.

"I want to know the favor."

"Cash first," retorted the leader.

She shook her head. He glared, taking a step toward her, but she didn't react. Showing fear would only endanger her further.

"What's the favor?"

The man sighed briefly, glancing toward one of his companions. This second man shrugged. The two of them muttered something, and then the leader said, "Find who's killing our patriarchs."

It was such a straightforward, direct request that Artemis didn't quite know how to respond. "Excuse me?"

He pointed at her. "Artemis Blythe?"

"Yes."

"We looked you up." He spoke in that gravelly, grating way that made her think of gargled glass. "You've helped the FBI," he said simply.

She blinked in surprise. This wasn't the line of questioning she'd expected. "I . . . er, no." She said quickly, "I mean, yes. But not anymore."

"Relax," he said. "We're not calling you a rat or nothing. We need to know who's been wasting our bosses."

"Your . . . what?"

"Old-timers. Old heads," he said. "Retired here. In Italy. Three of 'em."

"Three . . ." She blinked. "I'm confused."

He looked irritated now. "You stupid? Give me the cash and figure out who's wasting our bosses. Then, Tommy can live. Clear?" He leaned in now, his breath smelling of cigarettes and whiskey. "And Tommy isn't welcome back home. Ever. Got it?"

Artemis felt her stomach drop. She had been hoping for a simple exchange, but now it seemed like she had gotten herself into something far more dangerous than she had anticipated. She took a deep breath, trying to steady herself.

"I don't work with the FBI anymore."

He frowned at her. "So you saying no to the deal?"

"No, I'm saying you're changing the deal. Cash. I've offered what I can."

He shook his head. "Nah. Cash—boss has cash. His brother's son is dead. He says figure this out, and we'll figure out the rest. Life for a life."

"What do you mean life for a life?"

He smirked at her, flashing a golden tooth, but his features were so rigid the expression didn't reach the rest of his face. "I mean," he said conversationally, "you figure out who's killing our patrons, and we'll take care of the rest."

"I'm . . . I'm not going to hand someone over to you to be executed," she said firmly.

"Right, right," he muttered, waving a hand as if brushing her protests away. "So deal or not?"

"I'm still not sure what you think I can do for you."

He just shrugged. Twice now, she'd tried to deflect, but clearly, they weren't going to take no for an answer. Three old mobsters dead—that's what it sounded like. Did she really want to get involved in all of this?

Another murder investigation? She couldn't just hand someone over, could she? She wrinkled her nose. No . . . No, certainly not.

She bit her lower lip, feeling a rising sense of unease. Thoughts swirled through her, and another splash jarred her to her senses. She shrugged. "How do I know Tommy will be taken off the hit list, then?"

The man shrugged. "You just have to trust us."

Artemis let out a humorless laugh. "Trust you? You're a group of armed men who shot up our apartment."

His face twisted into a sneer. "Look, lady, you're in no position to argue. You either take the deal or . . ." He trailed off, but the implication was clear.

Artemis felt a cold sweat break out on her forehead. She had to get out of this situation, but how?

"I need some time to think," she said finally. "I'll come back with the cash, and we can talk more."

"No," he said simply. "No time. Take it or leave it."

She stared at him. He didn't blink. She swallowed, glancing over her shoulder once again and rubbing her hands nervously together. "I . . ." she trailed off. "Fine," she said at last, letting out a long breath. "What do I need to know?"

Before she'd even finished the sentence, though, the man was shoving something at her. She took the file from him.

"Figure out who did it," he said, his voice a low growl. "And next time, bring cash."

He turned away just as quickly, gesturing at the two other goons. The three of them, all wearing bright swim trunks, began to saunter away.

She watched as they disappeared around the corner, their footsteps clapping on the concrete. She was left standing alone, clutching the file tightly in her hands. Her mind was racing, trying to make sense of everything that had just transpired. She had stumbled into something dangerous.

But she couldn't just walk away. Her family was at stake.

She took a deep breath, steeling herself for what lay ahead. It was time to go to work. She flipped open the file and began to read. Her mind had the unique ability to retain whatever it read. She didn't forget. Her memory was both a gift and a curse.

As she walked away from the pool, her mind was already racing with possibilities. She would have to be careful, but she was determined to get to the bottom of this.

Tommy's life depended on it.

CHAPTER 5

THE SUN HAD LONG set on the sleepy northern Italian town as a thick fog rolled in, casting eerie designs against the cobblestone streets. The faint hum of cicadas blended with the distant tolling of church bells, creating an unsettling symphony that hung in the air like a haunting waltz.

In the heart of this somber scene, the dim lights of a small café flickered through the fog-encased windows, beckoning lost souls like moths to a flame.

Inside the café a dense cloud of cigarette smoke lingered above the patrons' heads, creating a haze that seemed to mute the already subdued voices. The scent of strong, bitter coffee mixed with the acrid smell of burning tobacco, painting a picture of quiet desperation.

Seated at a corner table near the back of the café was a young man, his plain attire doing little to make him stand out from the darkness that enveloped the room. The young man looked ordinary enough, but his thoughts were dark, and few would say anything different about his soul.

He observed the old man seated across the table, engrossed in a game of backgammon. As he studied the man's every move, a wicked glint flickered in his eyes, betraying his enjoyment of instilling fear in others.

The old man was terrified.

He'd been terrified ever since he'd come to this café earlier that morning. The plain-faced fellow smiled but hid it when the old man's wrinkled features turned toward him. The fear was evident in those eyes set above sunken cheeks.

The fear appealed to him.

It was a skill he had honed over the years—a secret pleasure he indulged in whenever the opportunity arose.

"Your move," the young man said, his voice hardly louder than the soft clatter of dice and the murmur of hushed conversations. The old man hesitated, his hand trembling slightly as he reached for a checker. With each passing moment, the tension between them grew more palpable, wrapping itself around them like a suffocating vine.

The old man's hands trembled as he moved his backgammon piece, the fear radiating off him like a force. Sweat beaded on his brow, and he wiped it away with a shaky hand, desperately trying to maintain some semblance of composure. Each breath labored, each heartbeat threatening to betray his terror.

"Ah, come on now," the young man chided, leaning in closer, his breath hot against the old man's cheek. "You can do better than that."

The old man swallowed hard, his mouth suddenly dry as the sands of the Sahara, his Adam's apple bobbing with the effort.

"You look nervous. What's got you so perturbed?" the young man said.

His companion hesitated and swallowed. "N-nothing." He shot a glance toward the door as it slammed shut, jumping in his seat.

Of course, the younger fellow knew exactly the source of his compatriot's consternation.

He'd caused it, after all.

"Tell me," the young man drawled, sipping his espresso nonchalantly, "do you ever wonder why bad things happen to good people?" The question hung heavy in the air, unbidden and so very unwelcome.

"Life . . . life is unpredictable," the old man managed to croak out, his voice trembling just as much as his hands.

"Indeed, it is," the young man replied smoothly, clearly relishing the older gentleman's discomfort. His gaze slid down to a crumpled white paper resting next to his coffee cup, three names crossed off with bold, decisive strokes. A satisfied grin spread across his face as his eyes lingered on the fourth name, still untouched but soon to join its brethren in obscurity.

"Sometimes, though," the young man continued, his fingers tracing the edges of the paper, "fate requires a little . . . assistance."

"Please," the old man whispered, desperation lacing his voice, "I-I have a family, children . . ."

"Ah yes, but so did they." He gestured to the paper with a flick of his wrist, as if the lives of those crossed-off names meant nothing more than a casual inconvenience. "You see, my dear sir, we all have our roles to play. And yours . . . well . . . will you play yours?"

The old man sighed, muttering to himself, crossing himself. As his finger wagged over his chest, though, the other man's hand shot out, catching it.

"Don't do that," he said, his voice a snarl. "God won't help you."

The older man winced, withdrawing his finger. He stared at the note with the names, mouth unhinged.

"The fourth name. Are you going to tell me?"

"Just . . . why? Why are you doing this?"

"Are you going to tell me?" the younger man repeated, enunciating each word with extreme care.

The air in the small café seemed to thicken with tension, the smoke hanging heavier than ever, as the old man stared into the abyss that was his future and found only darkness.

The old man, beads of sweat forming on his brow, stood abruptly from the backgammon game, muttering an excuse about needing the restroom. He moved slowly but with purpose toward the back of the café, as if trying to maintain some semblance of dignity.

"Ah," the young man murmured under his breath, a wicked grin playing at his lips. He rose to his feet, careful not to draw attention to himself as he slinked after the old man, his heart pounding with anticipation. All those hours of planning, all that meticulous preparation, were about to come to fruition.

He just needed the names.

One at a time.

His contact was giving them one at a time.

In exchange for his own life.

As he made his way across the dimly lit café, the young man couldn't help but savor the irony: this quaint little establishment, nestled deep within the heart of Veneto, would soon bear witness to one of the most sinister acts imaginable. And none of its patrons, blissfully unaware of the darkness lurking among them, would ever know the truth. It was almost poetic, in a twisted sort of way.

His eyes darted from side to side as he navigated the maze of tables and chairs, searching for any sign of interference. But the other patrons seemed wholly absorbed in their own affairs, their faces obscured by the lingering veil of smoke. He smirked. Just as he'd hoped.

The thrill of the hunt coursed through his veins like liquid fire. His fingers tightened around the crumpled piece of paper, the names of his victims taunting him from beyond the grave. They had underestimated him, just as the old man had, and now they were paying the price.

Please, he thought, imitating the old man's pitiful plea. *As if begging for mercy would save him.* He couldn't help but laugh, a cold, mirthless sound.

The dimly lit hallway leading to the restroom was narrow and shrouded in shadows. Flickering lights cast an eerie glow on the damp walls, giving the impression of a sinister tunnel that had no end. The young man could hear the muffled sounds of laughter and conversation from the café fading behind him, replaced by the steady drip of water through the corridor.

The old man's footsteps were slow and hesitant, betraying his vulnerability. A cruel smile played on the young man's lips, as he relished the fear he instilled in others.

"Can't run, can you?" he murmured under his breath, the words swallowed by the sound of his own pulse pounding in his ears. He knew this moment was crucial; every second counted as he stalked the old man through the darkness, each footstep bringing him closer to victory.

"Stop," the old man suddenly whispered, pausing at the entrance to the restroom. His trembling hand reached out for the door handle, but he hesitated, as if sensing the danger lurking just behind him.

"Something wrong?" the young man asked mockingly, his voice dripping with scorn. "Afraid of what you might find in there?"

He couldn't help but enjoy the old man's terror, even as he silently urged him to keep moving.

"Who are you?" the old man managed to stammer, looking around nervously, trying to catch a glimpse of his pursuer. "Why me? Why did you come for me?"

"Answers," the young man replied coldly, closing in on his target. "And I'm going to get them, one way or another." He could see beads of sweat forming on the old man's brow, glistening in the faint light. It was a sight that filled him with satisfaction—the intoxicating power of fear, an emotion he wielded like a weapon.

"Please," the old man begged, his voice quivering. "I don't know any others. It's been so many years."

"Wrong answer. Tell me the truth. Now."

The old man stared at him, stared at the names on the paper clutched in his adversary's tight grip. Then he released a long, pent-up sigh.

"Alright," he whispered. "Alright . . . But . . ." He swallowed. "Please. Don't tell them it was me."

CHAPTER 6

THEY MARCHED TOWARD THE most recent crime scene of an Italian mobster. Neither Artemis nor Tommy spoke.

The mist crept along the narrow country road, tendrils of fog wrapping themselves around the trees as if attempting to claim them for their own. Artemis's hair whipped about her face, the damp air causing it to cling to her cheeks and neck. Her eyes were sharp and focused, scanning the surroundings with an intensity that belied her calm demeanor.

Tommy walked alongside her, his steps light on the gravel beneath him, seemingly unfazed by the eerie atmosphere. His motorcycle jacket was zipped in the front now.

Neither of them had spoken as they took a taxi from the north of Venice into the rural wine country of the Veneto. It took them a little under an hour to reach the latest crime scene. Death seemed to stalk her footsteps, and Artemis couldn't seem to escape.

As they continued down the path, a faint buzzing sound pierced the silence. Artemis pulled her phone from her pocket, glancing at the caller ID before promptly silencing the device.

It was Forester. She knew he would be worried, but she couldn't afford any distractions right now. He'd insist on helping, and she refused to drag him into this. His arm had already been injured. She was still recovering from her own bruises.

"Artemis," Tommy murmured, his voice barely audible over the rustling of leaves and the distant hum of an approaching car. "Shouldn't you take that?"

"No," she replied simply, her gaze fixed on the road ahead. "It's better if I keep him out of this. He'll be safer that way."

Tommy nodded, understanding her reasoning without needing further explanation. They both knew the dangers that came with delving too deep into the world of organized crime.

As they ventured farther down the road, Artemis replayed the details of the case in her mind, her photographic memory allowing her to visualize each piece of evidence as clearly as if it were laid out before her. She'd already committed the file to memory in the taxi ride on the way here.

Three mobsters, all retired and with extensive criminal histories, had been found dead in shallow graves. The killer had left no witnesses, no fingerprints, and no apparent motive—just a trail of bodies that seemed to point toward something even darker than simple vengeance.

The mist grew denser as they walked, the world around them receding into a haze of gray and green. It was as if nature itself were conspiring to conceal the truth, providing a veil for secrets to hide behind.

This was the road the killer had walked. The crime scene was located in the copse of trees just ahead.

She was working without police, but some of the information in the file had been from police reports, suggesting the men Tommy had angered had access to all sorts of connections.

Artemis's keen eyes scanned the landscape, taking in every detail. The damp soil beneath their feet squelched softly with each step, a testament to the recent rainfall that had left the area shrouded in mist. With Tommy following closely behind, they approached an outpost up ahead, where two police officers stood guard, blocking the road that led through the small grove. Her pulse quickened at the sight of their uniforms, but she maintained her composure, knowing any sign of panic would only draw attention.

As they neared the outpost, she veered off the road and into the thick undergrowth, guiding Tommy wordlessly with subtle gestures. They moved like a silent breeze, slipping between trees and shrubs, aware that the slightest noise could betray their presence. Every creaking branch, every rustling leaf sent a jolt of adrenaline through Artemis's veins, heightening her senses and sharpening her focus.

The cops had glanced toward them but looked away again. This was a well-enough traveled path.

She could sense Tommy's unease beside her, his breathing shallow and strained as they navigated the treacherous terrain. Together, they crept around the perimeter of the police, evading the watchful gazes of the officers stationed there.

Finally, after what seemed like an eternity spent in tense silence, they reached the crime scene.

"This is it," Tommy whispered, staring at the muddy ground.

She nodded once. The shallow grave was all too apparent in the mist-enshrouded thicket. Muddy water pooled around the edges of the hole, and Artemis could make out the outlines of something heavy that had been moved from the hole. She approached the maw in the earth cautiously, her heart pounding in her chest.

The faint sound of the cops speaking on the other side of the tree line, by the road, drifted through the small space. She ignored it, forcing her mind to focus. Artemis studied the scene intently, her mind racing as it processed the myriad details that might hold the key to unraveling this deadly enigma.

Tommy's life in exchange for cash and clarity: the identity of a killer.

Could she really give the name to them? They'd murder the perpetrator, no doubt. She hugged herself, suppressing an anxious tremor and deciding to cross that bridge when she came to it.

She noted the disturbed earth around the grave, the frenzied manner in which it had been dug, as if the killer had been desperate to dispose of the body quickly. The shovel discarded nearby bore traces of the same urgency, its handle imprinted with muddy marks from the murderer's grip. Artemis's heart raced, the thrill of the hunt coursing through her veins as she cataloged each piece of evidence in her encyclopedic memory.

Though they stood at the very heart of the mystery, the fog that surrounded them seemed to grow thicker still, as if determined to shroud the truth in impenetrable darkness.

Artemis paused in the copse, her black hair blending seamlessly into the gloom as she withdrew a manila folder from her jacket. She opened it with the precision of a surgeon, revealing three photographs and detailed crime scene reports of the murdered mobsters. Her features were devoid of any emotion as she forced her thoughts to be analytical.

Tommy leaned in, his eyes scanning the documents as Artemis said, "These men were all retired mobsters, each with an extensive criminal history." The first photo showed the body of a man well past his prime, his graying hair matted with blood. "Ennio Caputo, 62, once a feared enforcer."

"Wouldn't be him without a few broken bones," Tommy noted dryly, pointing to the contorted limbs of the deceased mobster.

She winced at the gesture.

"I hadn't noticed that."

She swallowed, feeling distaste all of a sudden.

"Here's the second one." Artemis tapped another image. This time, it was a balding man with a thick beard and a gold chain tangled around his neck. "Dante Romano, 57, a former loan shark with deep connections in the underworld. He retired five years ago, but some say he still had his hands in illegal activities."

"Guess retirement didn't suit him."

"Finally, the third victim." She pointed to the last photograph, depicting a tall, gaunt man with sunken eyes and a thin, cruel mouth. "Lucio Moretti, 60, a notorious drug trafficker before he stepped away from the game two years ago."

"Seems like they all had plenty of enemies," Tommy observed, his brow furrowed. "But who would want to take them out now, when they're already out of the picture?"

Artemis pursed her lips in thought, her mind racing through every detail of the case. "That's what we need to find out. Whoever is behind this isn't just killing for revenge or power—they're sending a message. And I intend to decipher it."

The entwined duo of mist and fog, as if the ghostly remnants of some long-forgotten battle between air and water, enveloped the area. The sun, which had fought valiantly to penetrate the dense atmospheric veil, found itself vanquished, its rays reduced to mere wisps that barely illuminated the damp earth beneath. Each step Artemis took felt heavy, weighed down by the oppressive atmosphere of the crime scene.

"Artemis," Tommy whispered, his voice nearly lost in the hushed rustling of the trees. "Look at this."

He pointed to a shovel lying next to the shallow grave, its handle slick with mud. Artemis approached cautiously, her eyes narrowing as she inspected the tool. She was careful not to disturb any potential evidence—taking care to keep her hands to herself, but her keen gaze didn't miss a single detail.

"Think the killer left it?"

"Probably," she replied. Then she frowned.

"What is it?"

"Hmm?"

"That look—it's like when you figure out a move that Helen hasn't spotted."

"Oh . . ." she trailed off, still frowning. "Just . . . Notice the mud markings on the handle?" she murmured. "See how they're angled? The killer gripped it with their left hand."

"Left-handed, huh?" Tommy glanced around as if expecting the murderer to materialize out of the fog. "Does that help us?"

"Maybe," Artemis replied, her mind already whirring with possibilities. "It's just another piece of the puzzle. We'll have to see where it fits."

"Right." Tommy hesitated, then added, "You think we'll find this guy, Artemis?"

Artemis looked back at her brother, her delicate features set in grim determination. "We will," she vowed, her voice steady and unwavering. "Don't worry."

"I wasn't."

She nodded.

He hesitated. "So . . . two million? You really got that type of cash?"

"Don't get any ideas."

He flung his hands up, and he gave a high-pitched sound of protest, suggesting that had been exactly what he'd been doing.

Artemis pulled her phone from her pocket, the device looking incongruous against the gloomy backdrop of the crime scene. She carefully snapped several photos, ensuring each one captured the shallow grave and the mud-caked shovel.

"Got what you need?" Tommy asked, his voice hushed as if he, too, could sense the dark pall that hung over the area.

"Almost," Artemis replied, her eyes scanning the surroundings for any additional clues.

As they prepared to leave the crime scene, Artemis's keen ears caught the sound of voices drifting toward them on the breeze.

The two cops still stood by the gate, conversing in low tones. For once, luck appeared to be on their side; the officers hadn't noticed their presence.

"Stay here," she whispered to Tommy, her eyes never leaving the policemen. "I'm going to see if I can hear what they're saying."

Tommy nodded, his expression serious but trusting. He knew better than to question her instincts. Artemis moved silently through the undergrowth, the damp earth muffling her footsteps as she drew closer to the unsuspecting officers. She crouched behind a thick bush, straining to catch their conversation. Her Italian wasn't nearly as good as her sister's, but she'd brushed up on the flight over, and her ability to memorize words allowed her to decipher most of what was said.

"Can you believe this case?" one cop said, shaking his head. "Three dead mobsters buried in their own graves. It's like something out of a horror movie."

"Tell me about it," the other agreed, shivering slightly within his jacket. "It's bad enough we gotta be out here in this creepy-ass place. But to think there's some lunatic running . . . Gives me the creeps."

"Hey, at least we're not out here alone," the first cop replied with a wry smile. "There's safety in numbers, right?"

The fog seemed to cling to the trees, weaving its tendrils around each branch like a desperate lover. Artemis crouched low in the undergrowth.

"Did you know it was Loretta who found the body?" one of the cops said to the other. At least, that's what Artemis's limited Italian pieced together. Leaning against the hood of their patrol car, the cops' voices could scarcely be heard above the whispering wind. "She's as pretty as I remember."

A snort. "Don't get any ideas. She's taken."

"I know, I know . . . Still . . ."

Artemis's gaze sharpened at the mention of the name, committing it to her memory. Loretta—a potential witness, someone who might have seen something the cops had missed. A pretty woman and local by the sound of it. Should be enough to locate her.

Artemis and Tommy returned from the direction they'd come, both moving hastily at each other's side. As the two of them beat a hasty retreat, Artemis glanced at her brother.

"Loretta. She found this body. We need to speak with her."

"Do you have a last name?"

Artemis shook her head. "Got any contacts in the area?"

"Umm . . . maybe," Tommy said. "I can probably find her, yeah. Just . . . give me some time."

"We don't have time, Tommy."

"Fine . . . fine. Just—here. Let me borrow your phone."

He extended his gloved hands. She hesitated, but he clicked his fingers insistently, and she handed him her phone.

The two of them emerged from the misty woods, returning back to the dusty trail. Tommy dialed a number, his face ridged with concern as he placed a call.

CHAPTER 7

THE WARM, GOLDEN RAYS of the late afternoon sun cast a glow on the idyllic landscape as Artemis and Tommy arrived at Signorina Loretta's small home in the Veneto region of Italy. But Artemis found it difficult to appreciate the beauty as she kept glancing nervously down the street, searching for any lingering police presence by the woman's home.

Olive groves stretched as far as the eye could see, their earthy scent mingling with the faint, salty breeze from the nearby sea. It was an enchanting setting that fit the modest stone house with its ivy-covered wall, yet one marred by the dark events that had brought them here.

Tommy took the steps leading to the small home two at a time before knocking on the door. A moment later, the door creaked open, revealing Loretta—a young woman with a kind smile etched into her hesitant features.

"Buongiorno," she greeted them, her voice full of warmth despite the tremor that betrayed her underlying anxiety.

"Good morning, Signorina Loretta," Artemis replied in broken Italian. "We . . ." she paused, trying to remember the appropriate words. "We wanted to speak . . ." Her words jumbled together.

"English?" guessed Loretta, raising an eyebrow, her olive skin framing a hesitant smile.

Artemis's eyebrows rose. "Do you speak English?"

Loretta hesitated, then nodded slowly. "Little. Yes."

Artemis breathed a slow sigh of relief. She wasn't looking forward to practicing her Italian.

"We're working with the police," Tommy lied seamlessly, "and wanted to speak with you about what you saw this morning."

"If it's not too much trouble," Artemis added quickly. "We know how difficult this must be for you?"

The woman at the door sighed but quickly hid the expression. She nodded once.

"Ah yes. Please, come in." Loretta motioned for them to enter, her eyes darting nervously around as though afraid someone might be watching.

Artemis followed her into the cozy living room, cluttered with knickknacks and family photographs, while Tommy lingered by the door, keeping watch. As Loretta began to speak, it quickly became apparent that her grasp of English was tenuous at best. She stumbled over words and phrases, often switching back to Italian in a desperate attempt to convey her thoughts.

"Murder . . . bad man . . . frighten," Loretta stammered, her hands wringing together in distress. "I want help, but . . ." She trailed off, seemingly at a loss for words.

"Take your time," Artemis encouraged gently, observing the woman with sharp eyes that missed nothing. "We're here to help you, and we'll do our best to understand."

"Thank you," Loretta whispered, tears welling up in her eyes.

The tension in the room thickened as Loretta hesitated, her eyes darting around the room like a cornered animal. Artemis could see she was afraid, not just of discussing the murder, but also of the dangerous nature of the victim.

"Please, Loretta, it's important that we find out what you saw," Artemis urged gently, trying to put her at ease. "You mentioned in your police report seeing a figure near the crime scene. Can you describe this person?"

The small bit of the report that she'd been provided by the mobsters was like a key in a lock. Only the police would've had access to that information, and so Loretta seemed to relax a bit more.

She bit her lip, swallowing hard before speaking. "It . . . it hard to say. Dark . . . tall . . . I think man." She shuddered involuntarily, as if the memory chilled her bones. "I see only shadow. But . . . no car."

Artemis leaned forward, her interest piqued. "No car?"

"No."

"What do you mean?"

She hesitated.

Artemis guessed, "There was no car on the road?"

A quick nod, a smile.

"Nothing parked there? Are you certain?"

Another nod.

If there had been no vehicle nearby, it raised questions about how the killer had arrived and departed from the scene.

"Si, si," Loretta insisted, nodding vigorously. "I know all cars in village. No new car, no strange car. Nothing. No car. I run that path. No car anywhere."

Artemis mulled over this information, her mind racing with possibilities. She knew that killers often relied on vehicles for quick escapes, especially in small towns where transportation options were limited. The absence of a car suggested that the murderer might have planned their escape using a different method—or perhaps they hadn't left the area at all.

"Did you hear anything unusual that morning, Loretta?" Artemis asked, her voice soft but insistent.

"Only . . . footsteps," Loretta whispered, her face pale. "Fast, like running. Then nothing."

Tommy cleared his throat from where he stood by the door, glancing at his sister.

"Artemis, do you think it's possible there was an accomplice?" Tommy asked, his brow furrowed in concern.

"I don't know," Artemis said slowly.

"Then how did they escape without a car?" he pressed.

"Consider the terrain," Artemis said, her voice measured and analytical. "This is a hilly region with many footpaths and short-cuts. It's conceivable that the killer knew the area well enough to navigate it quickly on foot."

"Like a local?" Tommy suggested.

Loretta was wincing as he spoke, staring at him.

"Perhaps," Artemis agreed, her mind racing ahead of their conversation. "Or someone who had spent time here before. Someone familiar with the landscape."

"Could the victim have known the killer, then?"

"An interesting question," Artemis mused, her thoughts now focused on the possible relationships between the murderer and their prey. The question prompted one of her own.

"Loretta, did you know the victim?"

She blinked. "Know?"

"Did you know? See him? Know him?"

"Know! Oh, no. Well . . ." Loretta hesitated, wincing. "Signore was . . . not good man."

Artemis nodded. "So we've heard. So you did know him."

"No. But know . . . about."

"You knew of him?"

"Everyone here know of."

"So he was a bit of a local legend?" Tommy asked.

She hesitated. "What is this? Legend?"

"Like . . . a local celebrity," Artemis said. "A hero?" She winced, realizing the word didn't quite fit.

But before she could correct herself, Loretta shook her head fiercely. "Not hero. No! No. Very bad man." She frowned. "Everyone know, yes. But not hero."

"Do you have any idea who might've wanted to kill him?" Artemis pressed.

Loretta paused, wrinkling her nose. She shrugged then and shook her head.

Artemis shared another look with her brother.

"Anything could help," Artemis said.

"I no not know."

"How about anyone left-handed," Artemis tried, shifting track.

"Umm . . . my aunt. Left. She live in Brussels."

"Okay . . ." Artemis trailed off. She doubted most women would have been able to lug the man's body into the forest. Besides, the vast majority of killers were men.

Artemis paced back and forth in the small room. She said, "Is there anything you've heard about . . . other murders?" she said. She didn't want to lead the question, but her curiosity was piqued.

"Other?"

"Mhmm."

The woman paused and bit her lip. Then she shrugged. "No."

Artemis frowned, feeling now as if she was being stonewalled. But a second later, Loretta's eyes widened.

"Left hand?"

"Yes. Do you know anyone?"

"Si. Yes. Umm . . . graveyard?"

"There's a graveyard near here?"

"Yes. Man there . . . left hand."

"The man at the graveyard . . ." Artemis trailed off.

Loretta rattled off something in Italian, and Artemis's eyes widened as she placed the words.

"The groundskeeper?" she said. "He's left-handed?"

Another fierce nod.

"Thank you," Artemis said slowly. "If there's anything else you can think of, can I give you my number?"

Loretta replied, but Artemis's mind was already on the move. A left-handed man who worked nearby digging graves for a living.

Was it going to be that straightforward?

Stranger things had happened, especially when murder was on the line.

CHAPTER 8

THE SOFT PURR OF the taxi's engine faded into silence as Artemis and Tommy stepped onto the damp cobblestone path leading to the small graveyard nestled in the heart of the Veneto region. The sun had dipped below the horizon, giving way to a gloomy twilight that silhouetted the centuries-old tombs.

Tommy paid the taxi driver, but Artemis was far too focused on the task at hand to even pay much mind as the driver peeled away.

It was a place where time stood still, where the dead whispered their tales to the fog-laden air.

"Looks like we're not alone," Tommy murmured, pointing toward the caretaker's outbuilding near the entrance. The modest structure stood like an unwelcome sentinel among the graves.

Its weathered brick walls and moss-covered roof bore witness to countless secrets buried beneath the soil. A single dim light flickered through a window, casting eerie outlines on the ground.

Leaning against the wall outside the building, a young man puffed away at a cigarette, his left hand holding it aloft while tendrils of smoke curled around his fingers. He appeared to be in his twenties, dressed in a leather jacket and dark jeans, the epitome of casual indifference. But Artemis's keen eyes picked up subtle cues that hinted at something more. The furtive glances he cast around the graveyard, the way his hand shook ever so slightly as he brought the cigarette to his lips—these were signs of unease, perhaps even fear.

"Interesting," she mused aloud, her mind already calculating, fitting together pieces like a chessboard in her head. "He's left-handed."

The two of them slowly began approaching the gate that led into the cemetery. The man by the outbuilding didn't notice them yet. She studied the man for a moment, wondering if this was the caretaker. He seemed young for the job.

But this was their lead: a left-handed caretaker near the scene of the crime. A man who had given locals the creeps.

The moon hung low over the graveyard, casting an eerie silver glow on the weathered tombstones. The boughs of ancient trees swayed and danced in the cool breeze. A dense fog crept silently through the rows of graves, blanketing the ground with a sense of foreboding.

"Hopefully we're not waking the dead," Tommy muttered.

Artemis just glanced at him.

They pushed open the gate, and it creaked, drawing the attention of the man smoking the cigarette.

He looked up, his eyes scanning the two newcomers with a mixture of curiosity and wariness. Artemis couldn't help but notice the way his eyes lingered on her, taking in every detail of her appearance. It was a look she had grown accustomed to over the years as a female chess player in a male-dominated sport.

"Evening," she called out to him, her voice ringing out across the graveyard. The man took a final drag from his cigarette, flicking it away into the darkness before stepping forward to meet them. "English?"

He hesitated, then shrugged. "Tourist town, yes. English. You're not from around here," he observed, his eyes darting between the two of them.

"We're just passing through," Tommy replied, his voice low and even.

The man nodded, but Artemis could sense that he was still on edge, still unsure of their intentions.

"Che cosa vuoi?" said the left-handed man. As they approached him, he drew a second light and put it to his lips. His cigarette glowed like a malevolent eye in the darkness. He was clearly agitated, his fingers flicking ashes with a rapid rhythm.

"Non vogliamo problemi," Artemis replied calmly, her Italian rough but serviceable for now. She had always been adept at picking up languages, another skill that served her well in the dangerous world she inhabited. "We just want to talk."

"Parla allora," the man snapped, glaring at them with undisguised suspicion. His dark eyes darted from one to the other.

Artemis met his gaze unflinchingly, refusing to be intimidated by his hostile demeanor. Inwardly, however, she was calculating the risks involved in confronting him so directly. There was every chance he could be armed, but it was a risk she was willing to take.

She held out her hands as if to hold back a tide. "Are you alright?" she said slowly. "You look nervous."

She took another step toward him.

The man was growing more agitated the closer they came. He was waving a hand rapidly now as if to shoo them away.

"Leave," he said. "Now!" His eyes held something in them . . . as if he was pleading with them.

Her eyes flicked to the building behind him, then to the visible tombstones.

The tombstones in the graveyard looked like ancient sentinels, standing guard over the dead. There were crosses of all shapes and sizes carved into them, some with intricate designs that spoke of a long-forgotten time. The fog was thickening around them, making it difficult to see more than a few meters ahead. One of the nearest tombstones had an etching that she translated slowly, written under the jutting stone cross. It read, Come to me all who are weary and heavy laden . . . I will give you rest.

She stared at the tombstone, wondering if the person buried there had ever found the rest they'd sought.

Three Italian mobsters had been put to rest against their will.

The smell of decay hung around them like mist, and Artemis could feel Tommy tense beside her. She knew he was just as aware as she was that something wasn't right here.

The smoking man kept shooing them. "Leave!" he demanded. "I mean it. Go!"

She crossed her arms. "Sir, we wanted to ask you about the incident that occurred a few miles from here. I'm sure you've heard of it. Lucio Moretti is dead. Murdered."

She spoke slowly, watching his expression and reading his non-verbal cues to make sure he could keep up with what she was saying. Understanding her didn't seem to be an issue. The moment she said Moretti's name, his eyes widened in horror. He shot a frantic look over his shoulder toward the outbuilding and then pointed an accusing finger at her.

"Leave! Leave now! Go!" He picked up a shovel near the building, and it scraped as it moved across concrete. He raised it threateningly.

"Hang on!" snapped Tommy. "Back off, bud."

But Artemis just frowned. "What has you so concerned, sir? My name is Artemis. What's yours?"

"Jon," he replied simply. "Go."

"Not very polite, Jon. Do you dislike tourists?"

He hesitated, then nodded, tossing his second cigarette to the ground where ash trailed in a small arc.

"Yes," he said simply. "Now go!" He half raised his shovel again.

The man was breathing heavily, panic in his eyes.

"Did you know Mr. Moretti?" Artemis insisted, still confused by his openly hostile reactions. He wasn't acting guilty, but rather as if he was afraid for his physical safety.

Did he think they were here to harm him? If so. . .

She paused, wrinkling her nose.

She thought she heard some sounds coming from the outbuilding now, and she spotted a figure moving across the glass.

"Sir," she said slowly. "Jon—do you have visitors?"

But he just shook his head adamantly and waved a hand at them again. "Go!" he said. "I don't know Moretti. Never. Didn't hurt Moretti. He die this morning, hmm?"

"Yes . . ."

"I was with mother at church in morning." He shrugged. "Twenty people see me. I shake hand at door." He mimed the motion as if worried they wouldn't understand him.

"Can you give me the names of the people who saw you?" Artemis said slowly. He nodded adamantly. "Yes. Of course. Priest saw me. He is friend."

"What church?" Tommy insisted.

"The church of San Giuseppe," Jon replied, his voice still laced with tension. "Now leave. I don't want trouble."

Artemis exchanged a look with Tommy, then nodded. "Thank you for your time, Jon . . ." She trailed off, frowning, as he continued to scratch at his face with his left hand. He lowered the hand when he caught her looking, though, and frowned deeply.

"We'll check your alibi," she said quietly. "Did you see anyone on your way to church? Did you hear anything?"

They stood about ten paces away with the arms of the mist attempting to push them apart.

The man shook his head adamantly. "No! Nothing."

"Are you sure?"

He hesitated, his eyes flickering. "I . . ."

Artemis had grown up as the daughter of a mentalist. Her father had taught her to read human body language. And this man was hiding something.

She began to speak, but he quickly recovered and exclaimed, "Leave! Leave now! Go!"

"What did you see?" she insisted.

But just then, the source of the man's consternation made itself all too apparent.

The door to the outbuilding slammed open, none too gently. Four men, each one seemingly more red-faced and drunk than the last, stumbled out. They hadn't noticed Artemis or Tommy yet, but their gaze was fixated on Jon, and they spoke to him in Italian as they circled him.

Clearly, these men were no friends of Jon.

The largest of the bunch clapped a hand on the back of Jon's neck, squeezing hard until the smaller man yelped.

In Italian, he said, "You were hiding something, huh?"

He raised a small jewelry box, wiggling it under the man's nose. Behind him, through the door, Artemis spotted the outbuilding in shambles. These four men had been searching the place.

"So why did you kill him, huh?" snapped the big man. "This was his. I know this. He had this. You stole it." He squeezed his hand even tighter around Jon's neck.

Jon was protesting now, shaking his head furiously. "I found it!" he squeaked. "I swear, I found it!"

"Don't lie to me, Jon!" snarled the big man.

Now, as the mist cleared briefly, caught by a gust of wind, Artemis was given a clear image of the fellow in question.

He had a cruel, angular face, and his eyes were dark and calculating. He was the kind of man who thought nothing of using violence to get what he wanted.

Artemis could feel her heartrate increase as the situation became more volatile. She had no idea who these men were or what they were capable of. But she knew she couldn't just stand there and watch as they roughed up the caretaker.

Especially since he'd seen something. She needed to know what.

She cleared her throat. "Excuse me," she called out in Italian.

The drunken men didn't seem to hear her. So she cleared her throat. Tommy gripped her arm as if trying to keep her quiet. But she shook her wrist free and called out louder. "Excuse me!"

All of the men suddenly turned to her.

Their eyes were bloodshot. One of them had blood leaking down his hand and a piece of glass embedded in the skin where he'd apparently punched something fragile in the caretaker's building.

But now, all four men stared at Tommy and Artemis. The one with the angular face and dark eyes blinked once. Then he cursed.

Artemis held up her hands as if to calm him. She began to say, "We're just passing through, and we wanted to ask Jon a few—"

Before she could finish, though, the man yelled, drawing a weapon from his waistband. He glared, his red eyes shifting to slits as he pointed the weapon at her head.

"Who the hell are you?" he snapped in Italian. "Move, and I'll paint the ground."

CHAPTER 9

ARTEMIS FROZE, STARING DOWN the barrel of the gun. She hesitated only briefly, but then Tommy shouted, "Shit!" and her brother turned on his heel to run.

She yelled as he darted away.

The drunk thug blinked once, as if surprised his command to hold still had been disobeyed. Then he raised his gun and opened fire as Tommy dove behind a small stone fence encircling the graveyard. "Artemis, duck!" Tommy screamed.

He was waving his hand over his head if only for a few moments longer, as if to draw the attention of the gunmen.

Two more guns had emerged and were now raised.

The caretaker, Jon, had momentarily been discarded, shoved roughly backward, where he'd tripped over a tombstone.

Artemis was mid-motion as well. Tommy's distraction gave her a split second to fling herself behind a concrete slab before bullets were aimed in her direction as well.

Inwardly, she was vowing to kick Tommy in the crotch if they made it out alive. Why the hell couldn't her brother just think before acting sometimes? But the slew of scathing thoughts rising up were soon suppressed in a hail of bullets.

Artemis and Tommy ducked for cover in the graveyard as four drunken Italian mobsters—with guns blazing—sent a hailstorm of bullets in their direction.

"Damn!" Tommy cursed between gritted teeth, his voice nearly lost under the gunfire. He pressed his back against the stone wall, providing him with minimal protection from the mobsters' assault. Sweat trickled down his forehead, his eyes darting nervously from side to side.

Artemis spared her brother a glare, but it didn't last long as a new salvo of handgun fire erupted.

Just then, a bullet ricocheted off the tombstone inches from Artemis's head, sending shards of concrete flying. She flinched, gripping the edge of the tombstone for support. It wouldn't be long before her cover was destroyed entirely.

She had to move. She gestured at her brother behind her back, indicating this. He gave her a quick, panicked glance.

The shadows of the tombstones stretched long and slender across the moonlit ground, their twisted forms reaching toward Artemis and Tommy like spectral fingers. The drunken laughter of the mobsters grew closer, mingling with the sharp cracks of gunfire that punctuated the night.

They were walking toward the cover.

"Tommy," Artemis whispered, her eyes darting between the shapes of the approaching mobsters and their limited options for escape. "We're going to have to run for it."

He hissed but gave her a nod. "Me first."

"Wait," she began.

But too late. Tommy bolted.

She cursed as the men took shots after her retreating brother, but if there were ever an Olympic sport of dodging gunfire, her brother would've qualified. He'd spent more than his share of time fleeing either cops or mobsters.

But she didn't have time to offer up a prayer on his behalf. Instead, she turned and bolted, running deeper into the graveyard.

Tommy was drawing the gunmen away. Two of them were chasing after him now, having missed as he darted between thick old-growth tree trunks.

The other two were coming in her direction.

Artemis watched intently as the mobsters stumbled forward, their weapons wavering unsteadily in their hands. She could tell from their erratic movements that they were heavily intoxicated—their bravado bolstered by alcohol but their aim severely compromised.

She broke from cover. Bullets missed. She kept low, sprinting hard.

As she darted between crumbling crypts and ancient headstones, Artemis knew that their survival hinged on her ability to outthink the mobsters.

She raced deep into the mist-filled graveyard. Tall, metal fencing encircled her.

She crouched under cover, breathing heavily. She waited, listening.

She could hear the sound of footsteps drawing closer, the drunken slurs of the mobsters growing louder as they approached. Artemis's heart raced as she mentally prepared herself for the inevitable confrontation.

There was a pause, some hesitant shuffling, and then the men veered off. She hadn't realized she'd been tense, her hand gripping a rock. Just then, another hand touched her shoulder.

She nearly screamed, spinning around and biting her tongue to hold back the sound. She stared, bug-eyed, at where Tommy crouched near her, holding out his hands as if to calm her. He held a finger to his lips. "It's me," he whispered. "Shh."

She stared at him, then gave him a once-over where they both crouched in the mist and moon-shrouded dark near the tombstone.

"Are you okay?" she whispered.

He gave a quick nod. "They're coming back this way? Gave them the slip at the hedge, but they're not as dumb as they look."

Artemis's gut churned as she knelt behind the ornate marble tombstone. She clenched her jaw, suppressing the urge to admonish Tommy for his careless actions that had led them into this nightmare. Instead, she drew in a deep breath, forcing herself to focus on the task at hand: survival.

"Tommy, we need to keep moving," she whispered through gritted teeth, her voice steelier than she felt inside. "Further back into the graveyard. We can scale the fence. Stay low. Stay quiet."

"Right behind you," Tommy whispered, his own fear palpable.

With a final glance at their pursuers, who were still a few rows away and blissfully unaware of their precise location, Artemis darted from their temporary sanctuary, Tommy following closely on her heels.

For a moment, she thought they'd gone unnoticed. But a second later, a bullet whizzed past her ear, its high-pitched whine making her flinch.

"Damn it!" she hissed under her breath, her heart pounding in her chest like a drum. The mobsters were closing in, and their options were narrowing by the second.

As they rounded a corner, Artemis caught sight of a large mausoleum looming ominously ahead of them. The imposing structure was adorned with intricate carvings of angels and gargoyles, their stone faces seemingly mocking the pair's desperate plight.

"Shit!" Tommy said, coming to a stumbling halt in the shadow of the structure.

Artemis spotted the problem a second after her brother.

Indeed, the fence was up against the back of the tree line . . . But it was topped with barbed wire and twice as tall as the entry gate.

"Shit," Tommy said, even louder.

She couldn't help but agree.

"Artemis . . . we're trapped," Tommy gasped, his eyes wide with terror as they both realized the barbed wire gate was barring their exit route.

"Stop panicking!" she snapped, her frustration boiling over. "We'll find another way out. We have to."

"Okay . . . okay," Tommy stammered, trying to steady himself. "What do we do now?"

He was breathing heavily, concealed by the mausoleum wall and speaking in a near whisper.

Artemis's mind churned out potential solutions, but each of them was more dangerous than the last.

Now, she could hear the sound of approaching footsteps. The mobsters were drawing closer. They were like fish trapped in the bottom of a barrel, and the mobsters were the lid.

No way out.

"Let me think," she murmured, her hair whipping around her face as she surveyed their surroundings, searching for any possible escape route.

"Artemis . . ." Tommy began, but she cut him off.

"Quiet, Tommy. I need to focus."

As the mobsters' voices grew louder and their footsteps echoed through the graveyard, Artemis knew they were running out of time.

"We can hide on the mausoleum."

"That's the first place they'll look!" Tommy protested.

Time was running out. The footsteps were drawing nearer.

"Not in," she replied quickly. "On. On top of. Look at it," Artemis whispered urgently, waving a hand in its direction. "See how the gargoyles and angels protrude from the walls? We can use them to climb up and out of sight."

Tommy squinted at the stone edifice, then back at Artemis, his face a mix of doubt and desperation. But as the mobsters' voices grew closer, he nodded in agreement.

"Alright, let's do it."

Artemis moved first, her nimble fingers finding a grip on one of the angelic carvings. She pulled herself up with surprising strength, her body taut with determination. Tommy followed closely behind; he'd always been a natural climber, and Artemis was reminded of the time he'd scaled the side of a hospital to see her.

"Remember," she hissed down at him, "quiet and steady. We don't want to give ourselves away."

From their vantage point atop the mausoleum, Artemis and Tommy watched in near silence as the mobsters split up, their raucous laughter and slurred Italian drifting through the moonlit graveyard. The open malice in their voices made Artemis's stomach turn. She felt Tommy's breaths, shallow and heavy.

The mobsters kept coming closer, and the four of them paused, standing in the shadow of the gray structure. Two gunmen slipped inside, looking about, but then emerged a second later, both frowning and shaking their heads.

Neither of them looked up.

Artemis and Tommy hugged the gargoyles. One of the men waved a hand toward the fence. The leader of the group gestured back toward the road. His subordinates nodded, and Artemis watched as they split up. Two began to head toward the very back of the graveyard, and another two returned toward the entrance, moving fast and causing mist to sweep behind them.

Still, Artemis waited, tense.

She watched as the two gunmen searched the gate, the barbed wire. One was shaking his head in disgust, and she didn't have to hear him to know he was protesting that no one could've scaled it.

The two gunmen turned back around, stomping in the direction of the entrance once more, muttering to each other, their drunken stumbling forcing them to keep their eyes on the ground lest they trip over a tombstone.

Time seemed to slow as she analyzed the terrain and positions of the mobsters. She knew they had to act fast.

"Alright," she finally conceded, eyes locked on the two unsuspecting men. "On my signal, we drop down and neutralize them. Then we take their guns."

"Got it," Tommy murmured, his body tensed and coiled like a spring.

They waited, hearts pounding in unison, until the first two mobsters were far enough away, leaving this couple alone. Artemis gave a curt nod, and in one fluid motion, they dropped from the roof of the mausoleum, landing silently behind their targets.

"Buona serata, signori," Tommy whispered sardonically as he slammed his elbow into the first mobster's temple. He crumpled without a sound, unconscious before he hit the ground.

Artemis had snaked her arm around her target in a choke hold, using one of the submission techniques that Forester had taught her. He choked and grasped at her fingers, but Tommy darted over, punching the man twice and knocking him out.

She lowered this man to the ground as well.

"Got it," she replied, grabbing the fallen mobster's gun and expertly disarming the other man and handing this weapon to Tommy.

With the chilling cries of the wind as their only company, Artemis and Tommy made their way to the main building of the graveyard, armed this time. The moonlight on each gravestone cast ghostly figures on the dew-laden grass beneath them, and every step they took felt like a snare ready to clinch their ankles.

"Artemis, do you think the caretaker's still alive?" Tommy asked in a low voice, his gaze darting around.

"Let's hope so," she replied curtly, her mind focused on calculating every possible outcome. "We need all the help we can get."

As they approached the caretaker's cottage, its walls coated with ivy that rustled like whispers in the breeze, they noticed the door was slightly ajar. Artemis tensed, gripping her stolen gun tighter. She exchanged a glance with Tommy, who nodded, understanding the unspoken message: proceed with caution.

She spotted the two other mobsters moving about near the fence line, speaking to each other and shaking their heads.

With Tommy at her side, she slipped into the caretaker's cottage, searching for the only clue they had left.

CHAPTER 10

ARTEMIS AND TOMMY MOVED through the caretaker's building, and Artemis hooked the door behind her with her heel, shutting it in their wake.

For now, no gunshots—no shouts. The mobsters hadn't noticed them yet.

As the door slowly shut, Artemis allowed herself a faint breath of air. What had she even gotten herself into?

Inside the caretaker's building, she spotted a concrete partition that seemed to divide a living portion of the house from an office portion. On one side, there was a bed and a small kitchen. On the other side, a desk and a computer.

Artemis's gaze scanned the space. It was trashed—couches turned over, chairs splintered. The thugs had shown a small wooden jewelry box they'd discovered in Jon's possession, but there was no sign of the caretaker.

Artemis felt a flicker of fear on behalf of the man's well-being. She continued forward and then paused.

A sound was coming from down the hall.

"Look," Tommy whispered, his voice low and covert, as he pointed to an opening in a door at the end of the hall.

A second later, Artemis spotted it too.

Jon—at least he was still alive. The thin young man was attempting to sneak out through a window of the dilapidated building.

Artemis whispered his name, but he either didn't hear or pretended not to. He dropped out of the window. Artemis and Tommy hastened forward—she kept shooting glances over her shoulder to make sure the gunmen weren't in close pursuit.

They reached the window, and again she hissed after him, but Jon was moving, his footsteps crunching against fallen leaves. The young man was already moving further away, his lithe frame darting from cover to cover like a hunted animal.

Tommy and Artemis shared a quick look, then one at a time they slipped through the window as well.

Artemis's feet hit the ground, pressing into the leaves. She stepped off a fallen log, leaving a footprint in the green lichen.

Jon was still moving rapidly, not looking back—perhaps too scared to.

Keeping quiet as well, Artemis and Tommy trailed him at a safe distance, their senses heightened by the danger that lurked behind them. Still no gunshots—at least this was an improvement.

Suddenly, the young man skidded to a halt, pressing his back against a crumbling brick wall. His chest heaved as he fought to catch his breath, his wide eyes scanning the area for signs of pursuit.

He spotted them, and his eyes bugged. For a moment, it looked as if he might turn and run.

"Hey!" Artemis called out softly, stepping forward with her hands raised in a gesture of peace. "Non vogliamo farti del male. We just want to talk."

Jon hesitated, his gaze darting between her and Tommy as if trying to gauge their intentions. Then, with a swift movement, he held a finger to his lips, indicating the need for silence.

"Va bene," Artemis agreed, nodding to show her understanding.

"Follow me," the young man whispered in heavily accented English, his eyes still wide with fear. He took off again, this time at a more measured pace as he led them deeper into the heart of the forest.

Artemis's mind raced as they moved silently through the night. A small part of her was wondering if they were simply being led from the frying pan into the fire.

But another part of her wondered what all that had been about back in the graveyard. What had Jon seen? And what was that jewelry box?

They stepped from the forest onto a dark road. It led across a concrete path, and ahead, Artemis spotted the first row of Venetian buildings. They were heading south again, likely in order to lose any pursuit in the maze of streets.

The young man led Artemis and Tommy through the labyrinthine backstreets of Venice. Each narrow alleyway was a shadowy tunnel, punctuated by the occasional pool of light from a dim streetlamp, casting eerie patterns on the ancient cobblestones. The air was heavy with the scent of damp stone and the distant tang of seawater.

"Stay close," Artemis whispered to Tommy, her sharp eyes scanning their surroundings for any sign of danger. She could sense his tension beside her, his breath coming in shallow gasps as they moved deeper into the maze that was Venice at night.

"Turn here," the young man said, gesturing toward a particularly dark passage. They followed him cautiously, their footsteps sharp and distinct in the confined space. It felt as if the walls were closing in around them, but Artemis knew that getting lost in the city's twisted streets was their best chance of evading the mobsters who pursued them.

As they navigated the narrow corridors, Artemis couldn't help but think of Helen—where was her sister now? Was she safe?

The thought troubled her, and she pushed it aside.

Finally, they emerged onto a quiet, deserted street, the low hum of nighttime Venice fading to a hush. The young man seemed to visibly relax, looking around to make sure they were alone before turning to address Artemis and Tommy.

"Okay," he said, his voice barely audible. "We should be safe here . . ." He glanced past them, shifting nervously, his fingers fluttering to his neck where red marks from the mobster's grip could still be seen.

"I'm Jon Riccardo," he said slowly as if this should mean some-thing to them. When they didn't react, Jon tilted his head as if he were waiting for an answer from a slow child.

"Riccardo," he repeated hesitantly, still eyeing them warily. "As in the Riccardo family?"

"Riccardo," Artemis repeated, nodding. "Never heard of them."

He sighed, rubbing a hand over his face. "Suffice it to say, we used to be . . . how you say . . ." He waved a hand as if grasping for the words. Then he shrugged. "But . . . those people. They were members of the Riccardo family. And they're not exactly happy with me right now."

Artemis and Tommy exchanged a quick glance. They both knew that getting involved with the mafia was never a good idea. But they were already in too deep.

"What did they want with you?" Artemis asked, hoping to get some answers.

Jon hesitated, his eyes flicking nervously between them. "I . . . I don't know. They just said something about a box. But I don't have anything." He looked up at them, his eyes pleading for them to believe him.

Artemis studied him for a moment, then said, "We saw the box."

119

"Oh . . . yes, well . . ."

"We saw them find it."

He grimaced. "I may have . . ." He paused, then in the attitude of someone deliberately changing the subject, he said, "Right." Riccardo took a deep breath as if steeling himself for a difficult confession. "I . . . I saw something. It's not much, but maybe it'll help you."

"What about this box?" Tommy cut in.

But Jon Riccardo ignored him.

"Every detail counts," Artemis assured him, her mind racing with anticipation. If Jon had witnessed something important, it could be the key to unlocking the mystery that surrounded the godfather's death.

"Before the police arrived, I heard a scream," Riccardo began, his eyes darting around as if worried they were being watched. "I went to investigate, and I found the body . . ."

"Did you see anyone else at the scene?" Artemis asked, acutely aware of the importance of Riccardo's answer.

"Only for a moment," he admitted, biting his lip. "Someone was fleeing . . . on a bicycle."

"A bicycle?" Artemis repeated, her brow furrowing in thought. "That's an unusual choice of getaway vehicle. Did you notice anything particular about it?"

"It was a woman's bike," Riccardo said, his words tumbling out in a rush. "I know it's not much, but maybe . . . maybe it means something."

Artemis's dark eyes bored into the young man's face, taking in every detail as he spoke. The dim, flickering streetlight cast eerie lines across his gaunt cheeks, making him appear almost spectral. His thin hands trembled slightly as they gestured through the air, visibly struggling to find the right words amid the fractured mix of Italian and English that spilled from his lips.

"Please, signorina," the young man stammered, "I did not mean to cause any trouble. I only wanted to help."

Artemis wasn't sure she believed this part, but she glossed past it. "And this sound . . . when did you hear it?"

"Before the police arrived, I heard a scream," Riccardo whispered, his nearly disappearing in the distant hum of the Venetian nightlife. "A woman—she must have found the godfather's body first. I went to investigate, and I saw him . . . lying there."

"So a woman's bike . . . you're sure?"

"Si."

121

"You took the jewelry box?" Tommy insisted.

Riccardo sighed and shrugged as if he saw no point in denying it further.

"I took this from the crime scene," he admitted, his voice barely more than a whisper. "It was an impulsive act. I didn't mean to steal it, but . . . I thought it might be important. And I didn't want the police to have it. Old family habits . . . I'm not involved anymore," he said quickly. "Which is why those ones back there wanted me dead."

"Why try to keep it then?"

"Because . . ." He shrugged sheepishly. "It looked valuable." He gave a little half smile.

Artemis frowned, glancing at Tommy. The two of them stood at the edge of Venice, the trees behind them leading back to the misty woods.

"Why would an old man have a jewelry box in the woods?" she said quietly. "And why would the killer not take it?"

"Maybe the killer was distracted. Didn't think anyone would show up so soon," Tommy guessed.

Artemis hesitated. She shrugged briefly. "Maybe," she murmured. Her brow furrowed. "But if the box is valuable, why would the killer leave it behind? It doesn't make sense."

Tommy nodded in agreement.

Artemis nodded slowly, her mind already racing with possibilities. "We can't stay in one place for too long." She turned to Jon Riccardo. "Do you have any leads on where we can find this woman?"

Jon shook his head. "I'm sorry, signorina. I didn't recognize her."

Artemis sighed, feeling a sense of frustration. They were running out of time, and they had no leads. But she refused to give up. They had come too far to turn back now.

"Do you know of any left-handed women in the village?"

He shook his head again.

Artemis paused, testing her teeth. "Who might've wanted the godfather dead?"

He shrugged. "Many people. Many lives he ruined."

Artemis felt as if she were bashing her head against a wall with little in the way of movement. She was pacing on the cobblestone streets now, frowning as she did.

"Alright . . . well . . . What about these men?" She pulled out the file, showing the three dead men to their witness.

Jon hesitated, his eyebrows rising. Artemis made a mental note to check his alibi; perhaps he'd been lying.

But watching how he'd reacted to being manhandled by those mobsters, she didn't think so. And if not him . . . then who was killing these men?

Jon gave a sharp intake of breath.

"What is it?"

"They're dead too?" Jon asked in a voice that seemed to hope he had misunderstood.

"Yes. Do you know them?"

"The four horsemen."

"What?"

"The four horsemen," he repeated more insistently.

"What does that mean?"

"These men. These mobsters, they're killers." He paused, his gaunt face shifting into something of a grimace. He snapped his fingers as if straining for something. And then he nodded hastily. "Yes . . . yes, my grandfather."

"What?"

"Fourth. The fourth." He tapped the three pictures of the dead mobsters. "Four horsemen ruled northern Italy. About thirty years ago. They made Venice and larger Veneto the heart of their operations."

"And your grandfather?"

"Matteo Riccardo," he said quickly. "Yes. He is fourth. These three dead. My grandfather fourth."

Artemis stared. "If what you're saying is true, your grandfather might be the killer's next target."

Jon's face soured. Instead of looking alarmed, he looked indifferent. He shrugged. "My grandfather once tried to shoot me," he said simply. "Because I did not want to help him hide a body."

Artemis blinked. "Charming."

"No. Evil."

She sighed. "So where can I find Matteo Riccardo? If he's the next victim, we can find him to find the killer."

"I . . . I don't know. But I have a guess where he'll be tonight."

"Where?" "Venice," he said simply. "The float parade. It's tonight." "Parade?" Artemis said hesitantly.

He nodded, wagging his head. "Oh, yes." He even flashed a smirk. "It is something to see. Especially for a tourist. Just . . . be careful."

CHAPTER 11

THE NIGHT WAS ALIVE with a cacophony of laughter and music as Artemis and Tommy pushed their way through the throngs of revelers. Venice had transformed into a dazzling spectacle, where masked figures danced beneath a canopy of twinkling fairy lights, their vibrant costumes shimmering like a kaleidoscope of colors. Gondolas adorned with lanterns glided on the dark waters, carrying passengers who reveled in the enigmatic charm of the annual, masked float parade.

"Artemis," Tommy shouted over the noise, "you really think we'll find him here?"

"Matteo Riccardo is our only lead, Tommy." Her voice was unwavering, her eyes scanning the sea of faces obscured by masks. Artemis clutched at the picture given to her by Jon, examining it for the umpteenth time that night. It showed a man with a sharp jawline, high cheekbones, and piercing gray eyes—Matteo Riccardo, their target. She committed every detail to memory.

But as she scanned the throng of partying tourists and occasional locals, she couldn't help but feel they were swimming upriver. The plan was to find the fourth victim before the killer did. But how could they do that in a city full of masks?

The parade-goers swirled around Artemis and Tommy, a dizzying array of masks and costumes, rendering the task of locating Matteo near-impossible. Aristocratic bautas concealed faces behind stark-white surfaces; ghastly goblin masks grinned with demonic glee; delicate Colombina designs framed eyes that sparkled with mischief.

"One man, in this sea of anonymity," Artemis remarked, her voice tinged with frustration.

Tommy, who seemed to be growing more and more like his usual self as time went on, simply grunted. Then added, "Yeh."

"Where was the location Jon said his grandfather used to talk about?"

"The costume shop?"

"That's right. It was called..." Artemis trailed off, frowning and reaching back in her memory.

As she did, she was startled by a burst of fireworks overhead.

It seemed to jar her memory to the surface, and she snapped her fingers. "That's right," she said quickly. "A mask and costume shop called The Golden Mask. Let's head there."

Following the GPS on Tommy's phone, they made their way through the crowd, dodging dancing couples and giddy groups of friends. It wasn't long before they found themselves standing in front of a small shop with a golden Venetian mask hanging above the entrance. Its weathered sign swung gently in the night breeze, beckoning them forward. The storefront boasted a breathtaking display of colorful masks and intricate decorations that seemed to jump out from the darkness.

Artemis pushed the door open, and a bell tinkled overhead. The interior was dark, save for a few flickering candles and the dim light of a gas lamp. A faint, musty smell wafted from the shelves and displays lining the walls.

"Hello?" Artemis called out, her voice echoing in the quiet space.

No one answered.

The interior of the shop was dimly lit, with electric candles creating a pseudo-gothic ambiance. Masks of every shape and size lined the shelves, their vibrant hues and intricate designs drawing Artemis's eye. Her heart quickened as she considered the possibility that Matteo had sought refuge here, amid the very disguises that might hide his identity.

Suddenly, there was the sound of footsteps, and an elderly man emerged from behind a bead curtain.

He wore the logo of the store on his vest, and his features were creased in a smile.

"Beautiful, aren't they?" whispered the shopkeeper, his tone low and melodic against the faint strains of music drifting through the air. "Each one tells its own story."

"Indeed," Artemis agreed, her gaze lingering on a particularly ornate mask embellished with gold leaf and delicate filigree.

She turned back to the shopkeeper, her expression serious once more. "We're looking for someone—someone who might be hiding from danger. Have you seen anyone like that?"

"Ah, many people come to my shop—seeking solace, seeking disguise," the old man replied cryptically. "It is not my place to judge or question, only to provide."

She took a deep breath, inhaling the scent of incense that permeated the air, and focused her attention on the task at hand. She hesitated. She hadn't meant to be vague . . . but this man seemed to be enjoying his coyness. She decided to cut right to the point. "Do you know Matteo Riccardo?" she began.

The men leaned forward, as if certain he'd misheard her.

But before she could repeat the comment, her brother suddenly cursed from where he'd been standing by the window. Artemis's heart skipped a beat as Tommy tensed, his gaze locked on the shop entrance. She followed his line of sight and spotted two men striding by outside; one of them had a stony face and a hunched posture. A shiver ran down her spine; she recognized the mobsters who had previously targeted Tommy.

Mobsters from Italy, mobsters from Seattle. It was starting to feel like they were surrounded on all sides.

"Damn it," Tommy whispered under his breath. "They must have followed us."

"Stay calm," Artemis urged, her chest tightening with fear. "We can still make this work—we just need to be cautious."

The shop owner's eyes darted back and forth between them, his expression wavering between curiosity and unease. He seemed to sense the danger they posed, the potential for violence that loomed like a promise. In a voice like the husky whisper of a theater usher, he said, "If you are looking for protection, perhaps we can come to an agreement."

"An agreement?" Artemis questioned, her mind racing as she attempted to decipher his meaning.

"Si," the old man replied, leaning closer. "A small . . . compensation for my continued discretion."

She blinked. "Wait, what now?"

He waved a hand toward the window. "Friends of yours? No?" He smiled.

She stared at him, certain she'd misunderstood, but he was still smirking. She scowled now. "You're serious? You're blackmailing us?"

He just shrugged. The old shopkeeper didn't look nearly so jovial or genial after all. He was shaking his head. "You stay in here, yes? So . . . a small payment? Maybe two masks?" He grinned at her. "Thousand dollar each . . ."

"Just shut up," Tommy whispered. "I'm trying to hear them."

He was leaning forward, hiding by the concrete wall near the front window and straining to listen to the two men walking on the bridge outside.

Would they enter the shop?

It didn't look like it. At least, not yet.

"Very well," the shop owner hissed, eyes darting from Artemis to Tommy, then back to the mobsters outside. "If you don't want to pay, maybe I ask those gentlemen?"

Tommy's jaw tightened, and his hand moved instinctively toward his pocket, where Artemis knew he kept the gun concealed. Artemis began to protest, but her brother's hot temper acted first.

Her brother turned around, scowling across the counter. "Listen here," Tommy said, leaning in close to the man, his voice low and menacing. "We don't have time for your games. If you so much as breathe a word, I'll end you? Capisce?"

Artemis winced at the threat.

The shop owner's face paled at Tommy's words, and for a moment, Artemis thought he might back down. But instead, he took a deep breath and opened his mouth to cry out for help.

"Sono qui—"

Before the man could finish his sentence, Tommy lunged forward, tackling the shop owner to the ground. The man's head snapped back, hitting the counter, and he slumped over, silent.

Artemis and Tommy both stared.

"Is he dead?" she said, horrified.

"No," Tommy said quickly, sounding relieved. "He's breathing. See?"

Artemis let out a long breath of her own, watching as Tommy tugged at the old shopkeeper, hiding him from sight.

The shrill sound of the doorbell pierced the air, jolting Artemis from her thoughts. As the door swung open, a man stepped into the dimly lit shop. She was relieved to see it wasn't one of the mobsters outside.

This man, however, she recognized. He was impeccably dressed in a tailored suit, the fabric catching the soft glow of the candles scattered throughout the room. His face was bisected, partially obscured by a simple black half-mask, but she could still make out the left side of his face.

She recognized him.

Matteo Riccardo. The fourth horseman, the Italian mobster on a serial killer's hit list, had just wandered into the shop.

A second later, a man followed. He stood close to Riccardo, protectively, suggesting this second man was Matteo's body-guard. But that was where the affinity between them ended. Matteo was older, well past middle-aged. And the man behind him was young and enormous.

Both men were now quizzically looking around the store, no doubt searching for the man Tommy had just knocked out cold.

CHAPTER 12

MATTEO RICCARDO'S GRAY EYES studied Artemis, meeting her own mismatched gaze. The mobster's eyes narrowed, and his fingers touched the edges of his sleeves. "Where is Guy?" he repeated in slow, meticulous words. The Italian was jarring to Artemis.

She paused, swallowed, then forced a quick smile.

In one hand, her phone was out. Surreptitiously, she placed a call, hoping it would go through in time. She didn't raise the phone but kept it by her thigh.

She'd been looking for this very man, but now that she had him, she wasn't sure how to approach this. How did one tell a man like this that he was on someone's hit list? What if he thought it was a threat? What if he used his giant compatriot to shut her up?

She hesitated, taking in the situation as best she could. Her eyes darted around, searching. Matteo was tense. His sleeves were rolled down, but his fingers kept twitching against his leg. Her father had often told her that one could learn more about a man by how they acted rather than what they said. And this man was no exception. He kept shooting nervous glances over his shoulder. Not only that, but his right, masked, side was facing the door.

She paused only briefly.

But when the giant began to move past his boss to search the store, Artemis stepped in front of him. She couldn't risk them discovering the unconscious shop owner. Instead, she quickly said, "Sir, I'm sorry. Very sorry—but I think there's something you need to know."

The giant scowled now. His muscles bulged as he faced her, standing only two paces away, his head towering over a rack of masks.

Artemis could feel the weight of the giant's gaze on her, but she refused to back down. She had faced bigger and scarier men before, and she knew how to handle herself in these situations.

She took a deep breath and continued, her voice steady despite the apprehension she felt inside.

"Your name has been brought up in a conversation I overheard recently," she said, her eyes locked onto Matteo's. "It wasn't anything concrete, just some rumors about someone wanting to take you out. I thought you should know."

He stared at her. "Do I know you?"

"No, sir. My name is Artemis. But you are Matteo, right?" His hand twitched, but she quickly said, "I know you're hiding a pistol up your sleeve. But now I suppose you're aware someone is after you."

He looked surprised now, his wrinkled features going smooth as his eyes widened. "I see. Well . . ."

He adjusted his sleeves. He had the look of a man who wasn't quite sure what to do next. He studied her closely, frowning as he did. After a moment, he let out a long breath through his nose.

"Enzo," he said to his large bodyguard, "do you recognize this woman?"

A grunt and a shake of the head.

"You wouldn't," she said quickly. "I'm not involved in your line of work."

She kept her gaze on the men, but her attention was partially divided by a desire to check her phone, which still rested near her thigh. Time was ticking, and she could feel things coming to a head.

"And yet you seem involved. You also seem like exactly the sort of woman Giroud would date."

She hesitated. "I . . . I don't know that name." "Giroud? He's the one who's been killing my friends."

Matteo let the words sink in. He didn't pull his gun, but his tone held threat enough, and it caused Artemis to shiver.

"Giroud?" she said. "Does he have a first name?"

"Anton. But you might already know that, hmm? So where's Guy? Guy?" Matteo called louder.

Artemis winced as she thought she just vaguely picked up on the sound of a faint groan behind the counter. She quickly raised her hands, as if trying to corral a bull. Enzo, the giant, reached out, touched her arm, and began to tug on her.

Artemis winced at his rough grip. The giant pulled her toward his boss while Matteo looked on with a sneer. Up close, the giant of a man looked even more intimidating. His sheer size made her feel like a child in his grasp. But despite her fear, Artemis refused to show any signs of weakness. She kept her chin up and met Matteo's gaze head-on, ignoring Enzo entirely.

"Please, sir," she said. "I don't know where Guy is. But I do know that you're in danger, and I wanted to warn you."

Matteo's eyes narrowed. "And why should I trust you?"

She ignored the grip on her wrist, though it caused her pain. Artemis took a deep breath. "Because I'm not your enemy, sir. I'm just a woman who stumbled onto some information by chance. I don't have any motive to harm you or your organization. I just wanted to do the right thing."

Matteo considered her words for a moment, then snorted in scorn. "Even if I believed you, which I don't, three of my friends are dead. And you really do look like the sort of woman Giroud would date."

This name Giroud kept coming up—the man seemed convinced Giroud was after him.

"Guy!" Matteo called, his voice even more harsh as his eyes narrowed.

Enzo's grip tightened on Artemis's arm, eliciting a gasp of pain. But just then, the fruit of her earlier phone call arrived. She

140

spotted the figure moving hastily down the street in her direction, his own phone in hand. He paused, staring through the window.

Cameron Forester, ex-fighter and professional bad boy, had arrived on the scene, following her GPS-finder on her phone.

The moment he spotted the scene inside the mask shop, though, the tousle-haired ex-fighter blinked once, then cursed and broke into a dead sprint.

"Now you're going to tell me everything Giroud is up to," Matteo was saying, pulling a knife from his side. "And if you don't, I'm going to carve that pretty fa—"

Before he could finish, the glass door to the masks swung in and collided with Matteo's spine, sending the old man rocketing forward.

Forester didn't stop. Like a bull charging through a china shop, he barreled into Enzo from behind, knocking the giant of a man into a stand of porcelain masks. The masks shattered on the ground, spewing pieces every which way.

Enzo roared like a beast as he twisted around, re-righting himself and stepping over the toppled rack. He reached out with massive, banana-sized fingers toward Forester.

But Cameron had spent half a life in a cage, fighting large, dangerous men for a living. Men who'd trained their entire lives to learn how to kill.

And now . . .

Though Enzo was larger, Forester wasn't the type often given to fear. For one, he was a self-proclaimed sociopath. He didn't create the normal emotional connections that others did, but in addition, he also didn't feel fear the way others did.

And as Enzo surged at him, Forester stood his ground. The ruggedly handsome, tall agent shot Artemis a quick once-over, a question in his gaze. Are you okay?

But once he'd determined she wasn't harmed, his full attention shifted back to the lumbering galoot attempting to snatch at him. Forester caught the giant's lead hand.

"Behind you!" Artemis screamed.

Matteo was inching in, his knife at the ready.

But Forester had spotted the man in the reflection off the glass counter. And so, using Enzo's momentum, he twisted the giant's arm and sent him careening into his boss. Enzo knocked Matteo flat, and now the giant of a man was like a wounded animal.

He huffed and snarled, turning around again. This time, he lifted an entire glass display case over his head, howling as he flung it at Forester.

Cameron's eyes widened only briefly as he stepped aside, avoiding the case. The glass shattered on the ground as Artemis dove to avoid it as well. She ducked behind the counter with Tommy, snapping her fingers. "Where's the gun!" she hissed.

"Where's yours?" he retorted.

"Dropped it going out the window—who cares. Give me yours!"

Tommy reluctantly extended his toward her. "Clip is empty," he whispered fiercely. "We didn't take magazines."

Shit. She checked and realized he was telling the truth. But she still had to help Cameron, so she emerged from behind the counter with the gun in hand—no bullets, but the threat all the same.

The men locked in a fist-fight, though, didn't seem to notice or care. Forester had somehow managed to grab hold of Enzo's arm again and was now using the giant's momentum against him. He threw Enzo into the shattered glass display case, sending shards of glass everywhere.

Enzo stumbled back, his eyes wild with rage as he tried to regain his balance. But Forester wouldn't let him have it. He stepped forward and delivered a swift kick to the man's chest—sending him tumbling through the window.

Enzo crashed through it, shattering the remaining glass as he tumbled out onto the street below. The rest of them watched in stunned silence.

Matteo was slowly pushing up, grimacing as he did, blood trickling down the side of his wizened brow.

Cameron had a look in his eyes as he stalked toward the giant in the Venetian streets. A few tourists had spotted the commotion and were quickly distancing themselves. No phone cameras yet . . . though it was just a matter of time.

"Don't move!" Artemis snapped, pointing her unloaded gun directly at Matteo.

His hand gripped his knife, but his teeth set together as he spotted her weapon aimed at his head. He hissed at her in frustration.

Forester was stalking toward the giant, stepping through the shattered window. Cameron had a look in his eyes like death itself. Sometimes, he got like this. Especially when protecting

Artemis—there were few things he didn't joke about or find amusing.

But putting her in harm's way? That was a dangerous thing to trigger.

Cameron often didn't consider his own safety in such moments. "Careful!" she shouted.

Enzo had been lying on the ground, but as Cameron drew near, the large man swung out a massive, tree trunk–sized leg, sweeping Cameron's own.

Forester hit the ground hard, next to the giant.

Matteo cursed. Artemis took a step forward, but the knife-wielding mobster still blocked her path.

"Drop it!" she demanded, her gun pointed squarely at Matteo's face. He snarled at her.

Her eyes darted over his well-tailored suit shoulder.

Enzo had Cameron in a headlock, and the two were wrestling around. Cameron was trying to break free, but he didn't seem to be making much progress. And then, seemingly out of nowhere, with a flourishing twist of the hips, Forester managed to get his footing and shove the giant away from him.

Enzo stumbled in, crashing back through the shattered window, into the wall of masks behind him. The wooden frames shook as they hit the ground. A shower of glass beads rained down as broken porcelain faces stared up at them from the floor.

Enzo roared again and charged forward, but this time Cameron was ready for him. He stepped aside and kicked Enzo's feet out from under him, sending him tumbling down onto the broken pieces below.

The giant scrambled up quickly, though, snatching an armful of masks off the wall before turning back toward Forester—this time with a makeshift shield held in front of him.

Cameron smirked as he brought his fists up in a defensive stance once more.

"Stop!" Artemis commanded. "Stop, or I'll shoot him!"

A lie. A bluff.

But the men paused.

Enzo glanced over sharply, realizing his boss was in danger, caught in the sights of a woman with a gun. Matteo seemed less concerned. Perhaps he could sense Artemis's hesitation. Or perhaps he had faced more than one barrel in his life.

Now, though, the two men, covered in scrapes and bruises, were both breathing heavily. Cameron's right arm hung limply at his side, and Artemis realized he still had his cast on, though no sling. She winced in sympathy. But she couldn't afford to show it. Instead, she kept her gun trained on the two men. "I really am trying to help!" she snapped.

Matteo stared at her and blinked in surprise.

"Pull the trigger then," he sneered. "If that's what Giroud wants; not man enough to do it himself?"

But Artemis sighed, huffing in frustration. She shot a quick look to make sure Cameron was safely away from Enzo. At least the two men had stopped hammering each other, but the shattered glass and the commotion would've prompted undue attention. Eventually, the cops would show up. They needed to leave.

Artemis said, insistent, "Do I look like I'm trying to hurt you?"

She then lowered the gun, placing it on the counter behind her. Another bluff. But also one that was designed to earn goodwill. He didn't know it was an empty weapon.

Matteo watched her, his suspicion melting somewhat by a quizzical twitch of a white eyebrow. He stared at her, then adjusted his suit, wiped a thin bead of blood from his forehead, and said, "You really came to warn me? Why?"

"I'm trying to find who did this," she insisted.

He nodded. "Are you with the Riccardo family?"

She shook her head. "No. Independent."

He stared at her. "Who hired you?"

She huffed in frustration. "We can't talk here. We need to leave. Who's Giroud?"

"You really don't know?"

"No!"

Forester was still eyeing her, his eyebrow quirking up in a question. I'm fine, she mouthed toward him. He relaxed a bit.

Tommy had now emerged from behind the counter, smoothing long bangs back into a ponytail and adjusting his leather jacket. He frowned at Matteo, and Enzo growled, stepping forward to intercept him.

"He's not going to hurt you either!" Artemis said quickly. "Please, just listen."

Matteo snorted. "You make a compelling case." He glanced at the shattered glass, at the blood on his finger, and then at the gun she'd set on the glass counter.

"So you want to talk? Let's talk."

"Who's Giroud," she repeated.

Her ears remained strained for the sound of sirens, but there was a chance the police might not use them. She knew they were up against a clock.

"An asshole." "Be more specific."

"A huge asshole."

She sighed. "I'm trying to help."

"I don't know you!" he snapped.

"I'm the one who didn't shoot you."

Matteo sighed, and she could see the mobster wrestling with the desire to give control over . . . A man so used to being in charge, she doubted it was easy for him to try and let his guard down.

Finally, he said, "Giroud, if you really don't know, used to work for me. He blames me for his father's death. Blames all of us."

Artemis stared. "And?"

"And . . . All four of us." "The four horsemen?"

He snorted. "I never did like that stupid name."

"So Giroud is the one who you believe is going after you?"

"He said he would. On national television," Matteo retorted. "You really don't know, do you?"

Artemis blinked. "On . . . national . . . What?"

Matteo sighed. "Look it up. And in the meantime, stay the hell out of my way." Switching to Italian, the old mob boss gestured to his bodyguard, and Artemis caught snippets that sounded something like, "Enzo—hurry . . . three minutes . . . We must go."

The two men slipped past Cameron, issuing glares but nothing more. Artemis watched them leave, feeling a sinking sensation in her stomach. A death threat issued on national television? What had she gotten herself into?

CHAPTER 13

"YOU DIDN'T TAKE MY call," Forester said for what felt like the twentieth time.

Artemis sighed, massaging the bridge of her nose as she sat in the back of the car he'd borrowed. They were just north of Venice, moving slowly on old, crumbling streets.

Tommy now had the unloaded gun and had decided to regroup with them, to help protect his family.

Artemis hadn't thought this was a good idea, but Forester had refused to leave her side again. In the end, Tommy's constant insistence had worn her down.

She didn't like the thought that they might lead the mobsters right to Helen's doorstep, but on the other hand, perhaps keeping Tommy out of the way and on the down-low would be the best for everyone involved.

Now, though, she was weathering a different type of storm.

"I'm sorry," she said, the words now numb on her lips.

Forester's hand gripped the steering wheel, glaring through the windshield. His right arm was back in the sling, the cast visible in the glow from the moon extending through the windshield.

She loosed a small, sad sigh. "I wanted to keep you safe," she murmured.

"What was that?"

She repeated it, louder. He blinked and stared in the mirror, hesitating as if somehow something wasn't computing.

"Me?" He scowled. "That's my job. To keep you safe."

She glanced at him then back to her phone in her hand. "It's a two-way street, Cameron. I've dragged you halfway around the world. Put you in danger. I've ruined your job, and who knows if the FBI is after us or not."

"They are." "Right."

"So?" he said.

She blinked. "So . . . I've ruined your life!" As she said it, it came with a burst of emotion, and her eyes welled up. She wasn't sure where the feelings were coming from, but she knew they were true.

Forester looked as if he'd been slapped. He didn't care about the phone she held. On the device, they'd been looking up Giroud and his statement on national television about hunting the four horsemen.

But while Artemis had been swiping on her device to find the video, the two of them both went still now. Lost in silence.

Cameron said, in a low, soft voice, "I hope you don't really believe that."

"Hmm?" "You haven't ruined my life, Artemis. You've given it back to me."

He stared at her, meeting her eyes in the mirror. He had a soft expression now.

It was said, by some researchers, that sociopaths could occasionally bond with one or two primary relationships. Like a key that might unlock certain emotional depths. And in Cameron's case, it had been his deceased wife, a woman who'd been killed by a vengeful psychopath they'd escaped not too long ago.

She let out a faint huff of air, allowing it to lift her bangs like dandelion fluff.

Cameron continued in that slow, calm voice of his. "You've given me a new life. I wouldn't know what to do without you." He braced his off arm against the wheel, holding it briefly as he reached out with his hand to touch her.

The rough callouses on his finger and the warmth of his palm were reassuring. She could feel the faint tremor in his fingertips, the vibration of the car as they rolled along Italian streets, away from Venice.

The silence hung heavy in the air, but it was a comfortable silence. A silence that spoke volumes. Artemis could feel the weight of Cameron's hand in hers, grounding her. He was right. They had been through so much together, and in some ways, they had saved each other. They had been through hell and back, but somehow they had come out on the other side, and that was something to be grateful for. "You're not alone in this, you know," he said softly. "We'll figure this out together."

She nodded, feeling the knot in her chest loosen. She knew it wouldn't be easy, but with Cameron by her side, she felt like she had an anchor in the storm.

The car slowed down, and Cameron pulled into a small alley-way. They parked the car, and Cameron turned to her, his eyes serious.

"We need to talk about what we're going to do next," he said.

She nodded. "We need to figure out who this Giroud fellow is. If he's the killer, then I can give his name . . ."

She trailed off. "His name?"

"It's what they want," she said simply. "The mob. The ones chasing Tommy."

"The ones who shot up the apartment?"

"Yeah. They want two million dollars and the name of a man who's been knocking off old mobsters."

He stared at her. "You serious?"

"Mhmm."

"Shit, Checkers." He grinned. And a second later, he threw back his head and started laughing.

It wasn't a cynical laugh but a good-natured, well-humored one.

She found it somewhat contagious, to see Cameron laugh in the face of such things. She waited until he was done and allowed herself a small smile.

"Better?" she said.

"Yeah," he replied, chuckling. "Trust you to get involved with the mob in Italy."

"Trust me?" she said, raising her eyebrows. She sighed. "I mean . . . it's not that funny."

"It's a little funny," he said, holding up his fingers as if to say just a pinch.

Artemis tried to suppress a smile but couldn't help but let out a small chuckle. "Okay, maybe it's a little funny," she said, shaking her head.

Cameron's grin faded as he grew serious once again. "But we need to be careful. If the mob is involved, we're in deep shit."

"I know," Artemis said, her smile dropping as well. "But we can't just give them what they want. If I give them a name . . . they'll kill him."

"But we need to figure out a way to protect ourselves and Tommy. And we need to find out who this Giroud guy is. One step at a time."

"Yeah . . ." She returned her attention to the phone, scrolling through the search results. And then she stopped.

"I think I found it," she said. "Death threat issued by local hero . . . that's what it reads. It's translated."

"What does it say?"

Artemis clicked the link to the video and allowed the subtitles to play. As they did, she narrated for Cameron, watching the video.

On the screen, an emotional man was standing by a toppled electrical pole. The man was waving a finger at the camera, but it wasn't a gesture like a nun scolding a misbehaving miscreant. Rather, it was a violent motion, almost like a conductor or perhaps a dictator rousing an audience.

The man in the video was speaking in a loud voice, and with the help of the translated subtitles, Artemis was able to interpret what he was saying.

". . . four of them. Four dominate northern Italy. But not under my watch. This is going to end. Elect me, and it will be over."

He was speaking even more loudly now. Shaking his head as he did.

The man in the video had dark hair streaked with flecks of white. He wasn't handsome, but neither was he bad-looking. Rather, he was rugged, with a strong jawline and piercing eyes.

Something in those eyes had a haunted quality, though. And his voice creaked as he said, "And now . . . now, we all know how it turned personal."

He paused as if recovering from something. Behind him, a few men and women in suits watched, their eyes searching his as if looking to their leader for reassurance.

The man's voice cracked as he addressed the camera. His eyes weren't piercing, Artemis realized. No . . . that wasn't it. They were iron. A rigid, unyielding quality to his gaze.

He was beginning to get more emotional as he spoke. His voice cracked, and for a moment, it was as if a mask had slipped. A flash of rage creased his features, and his lower lip turned up in a snarl. He was shaking his head, side to side, and his voice shook as he called out, "The bastards killed my brother Timothe. I know you all saw the news."

A woman at his side reached out, touching his arm as if warning him he was heading into uncharted waters, but the man ripped his hand away.

He stared at the camera, pointing his finger at the lens. "I will make them pay," he said simply. "They will pay."

His voice was a low growl, and his eyes flashed with a barely concealed storm of fury. He let out a barking laugh. His finger was still waving about.

The woman at his side tried to touch his arm again, but he pulled sharply away. "I don't care if I don't eat or don't sleep. Those four bastards are going in the ground. Hear me? I know you did this. I know it was you."

He was staring into the camera now, and Artemis felt as if he were staring into her soul.

"You will see me coming. I want you to fear it. Fear me. Like my brother feared. You will suffer. I swear it."

And then the man turned away, marching stiffly back down a platform, his jacket billowing behind him. The video cut short.

Artemis spotted a few comments, the usual internet fare. She shook her head—anyone who spent a second on the internet didn't struggle with the question 'Are humans basically good?' That was answered within a few paragraphs on video comment feeds.

She knew the evil that lurked in a human heart, but she also knew the good that could be matured there.

But what was good?

A question that men like Giroud attempted to answer.

The political sort often had some sort of crusade, but now . . . Artemis wondered if he'd gone beyond the political realm. Had he been behind the murders?

"He's not left-handed," she said simply.

"How's that?"

"Giroud isn't left-handed. And Jon said he spotted a woman's bike fleeing the scene of the crime."

Forester grunted. "Where does that leave us?"

"He could have hired someone," Artemis said softly. "I don't know if I've ever seen anyone that angry . . ."

She paused, glancing at Forester.

This wasn't strictly true. He had been this angry. He'd attempted to kill the man who'd killed his wife.

Artemis let out a long, shaking sigh.

"Is . . ." she trailed off. "Are you okay?"

He blinked. "What? Me? Yeah, why?" He glanced at the video, then back at her again. He snorted. "Oh, this? Psh. I don't care. You do what you have to. I've got your back either way."

She smiled again, and this time it wasn't one of amusement but of gratitude.

"Got an address for this Giroud guy?"

"Coming in now," Artemis said, nodding. "Head west. He's not far."

Forester put the car in gear once more, and they began to pull away. As they did, he shot her a look. "Think we're going to have to break into the guy's house? Doubt he's taking guests this late."

Artemis gave a small shake of her head. "We'll see . . . We don't know he's involved."

"That video? He certainly looks involved. I don't think he's shedding any tears over their deaths."

Artemis frowned but didn't disagree.

She turned her phone onto the armrest between the seats, allowing the GPS to illuminate the dark, cramped space. They sped along old nighttime roads still swirling with mist, moving into the heart of Italy.

Mobsters on one side, killers on the other. Artemis could only hope they all made it out alive.

CHAPTER 14

THE MOON'S PALE LIGHT barely pierced the thick veil of clouds that shrouded the sky, leaving Giroud's isolated villa and its surroundings cloaked in an almost impenetrable darkness. Shadows clung to the ancient stone walls like a second skin, hinting at secrets buried deep within their weathered surface. A chill breeze whispered through the trees, stirring the leaves into a restless dance and adding to the unsettling atmosphere that permeated the estate.

Artemis stood by the gate, her raven black hair and loose, dark clothing blending seamlessly with the night. As she observed the benighted villa before her, her mind worked tirelessly, analyzing every detail, playing out countless scenarios as she sought the most advantageous course of action.

"Forester," Artemis whispered, her voice faint above the rustling leaves. The tall man appeared soundlessly beside her. He nodded toward the intercom mounted on the gatepost. "If you insist on playing nice," he muttered.

Taking a deep breath, Artemis pressed the intercom button. She waited, straining her ears for any sign of response, but only silence met her efforts. Frowning slightly, she tried again, speaking loud and clear, "Hello? Is anyone there?"

This time, a muffled Italian curse erupted from the speaker, followed by a sudden click as the connection was severed. Artemis's eyes narrowed.

"What was that word?" Forester asked. "It wasn't nice, was it?"

"No," she said with a sigh. "Looks like we'll have to do it the hard way."

Forester's eyes gleamed with mischief, a grin tugging at the corners of his mouth. "You know, I haven't had this much fun in a while," he whispered, rubbing his scarred palms together in anticipation.

Artemis shot him a cautious glance. "What? Breaking and entering?"

"Tomato. Tomato," he said.

"We're trying to catch a killer, Cameron."

"Of course," he replied, still grinning. "But that doesn't mean we can't enjoy ourselves a little, does it?"

Rolling her eyes, Artemis ignored his enthusiasm and turned her attention to the formidable gate that barred their way. The wrought iron bars twisted and twined like serpents, creating intricate patterns that seemed to writhe in the moonlight. She studied them for a moment, her hair lying over one shoulder as she tilted her head, considering the best way to proceed.

"Give me a boost," she finally instructed, nodding toward the gate.

"Your wish is my command," Forester said, his tone playful but obedient. He cupped his hands together, providing a makeshift step for Artemis. With his help, she managed to hoist herself up and over the gate, landing gracefully on the other side.

"Nice work," Forester murmured, following her lead and scaling the gate with impressive agility. Once they were both inside the villa grounds, Artemis allowed herself a brief moment of triumph before refocusing on the task at hand.

"Alright, let's find a way in," she whispered, her heart pounding in her chest as they crept closer to the imposing mansion. Every footfall felt unbearably loud, every breath a potential giveaway to their presence.

"Look there," Forester said softly, pointing to a ground-floor window obscured by an overgrown hedge. "Might be our best bet."

"We need to be quick and quiet."

"Piece of cake," Forester assured her, his grin never wavering as he pulled out a hard plastic credit card. Within moments, the latch clicked open, and they carefully pushed the window up just enough to slip inside.

"Remember," Artemis warned, her voice barely more than a breath, "we're here for evidence, nothing more. We can't afford any mistakes."

"Understood," Forester said, his eyes glinting with excitement. "Now let's see what secrets this place is hiding."

The darkness inside the mansion enveloped Artemis and Forester like a shroud, wrapping itself around them with an almost tangible quality. It was as if they had stepped into another world, one where all the familiar rules no longer applied. Here, in this murky realm of deception and silence, their senses were both heightened and dulled in equal measure.

"Can't see a damn thing," Forester muttered. "Feels like I'm blindfolded."

"Shh," Artemis admonished him, her fingers fumbling for the flashlight in her pocket. She hesitated for a moment, considering the risk of revealing their presence, then clicked it on, the beam cutting through the void like a knife. "Keep your voice down."

Forester nodded, chastened, as they began to navigate the labyrinthine hallways, guided by the narrow circle of light that seemed to shrink with each step they took. The darkness pressed in on them from all sides, suffocating and disorienting, its weight growing heavier with every passing second.

"Here," Artemis whispered as they entered what appeared to be a study, her flashlight illuminating a sleek computer atop a polished mahogany desk. "This could be our best chance at finding something."

"Let's hope Giroud hasn't password protected everything," Forester said, barely containing his excitement.

"Then we'll just have to be resourceful, won't we?" Artemis replied, her mind already racing ahead as she sat down at the computer and powered it on. The screen flickered to life, casting an eerie blue glow over the room, and she felt a surge of adrenaline course through her veins.

"Keep an eye out," she murmured, her fingers flying over the keys as she began her search. Each click was like a gunshot in the silence, and she winced at the noise, praying it wouldn't betray them.

"Come on," she muttered under her breath, her mind working at breakneck speed as she navigated the unfamiliar system. "There has to be something here . . ."

"Any luck?" Forester asked, his voice tight with tension.

"Give me a moment," Artemis said tersely, her concentration absolute. She had always been a problem solver, able to find solutions where others saw only dead ends. And now, more than ever, she needed that skill.

As the minutes ticked by, the pressure mounted, becoming almost unbearable. The sound of Forester's breaths, heavy with anticipation, filled the room as Artemis clenched her jaw, sifting through her mental archive for a clue that could unlock Giroud's computer.

She tried the birth year she'd seen in the online article. Nothing.

She tried his election year. Also, nothing.

She frowned, straining, forcing herself to calm and think logically. A memory surfaced—Giroud's brother.

She entered the name of the murdered younger brother, Timothe.

A blue light, the screen flickering.

To her immense relief, the computer granted her access, displaying folders and files across the screen. She couldn't help but feel a surge of satisfaction at her success.

"Got it," she announced, her voice laced with triumph. "Now let's see what we can find."

As her eyes scanned the screen, she quickly opened any file that seemed relevant to their investigation. With each passing moment, the tension in the room grew, like a ticking bomb waiting to explode.

"Anything damning?" Forester asked, his voice taut with anticipation.

"Nothing yet," she replied, her focus unwavering. "Usual emails. Business. Some articles about the dead mobsters. He's happy about it, but . . ." She frowned. "In these emails, he almost looks surprised."

"Could be a cover . . ."

"Maybe . . ." she trailed off, noticing a folder. She clicked on a file labeled Schedule, revealing a meticulous calendar of appointments and meetings. "According to this, Giroud had early morning engagements on all the days the murders took place."

"Damn," muttered Forester, disappointment evident in his tone. "So he was definitely finding an alibi."

She hesitated. "Two of these meetings were public. There'd be records if he wasn't there."

"So . . . what? Giroud's not our guy?"

"Matteo was wrong," she muttered.

"Shit. So . . . we're looking for someone else?"

"Looks that way," Artemis confirmed, her mind racing with the implications of this discovery. It wasn't *impossible* that the politician had hired a hitman to do the actual killing, but Artemis didn't buy it. She had seen the rage in Anton Giroud's speech. He would want to be there, to see them punished for what they did to his brother, Timothe. But if Giroud wasn't the killer, who was? And what would they do now?

"Let's keep looking," she suggested, unwilling to give up on their search just yet. As she dug deeper into Giroud's digital footprint, she couldn't shake the nagging feeling that something wasn't quite right. But for now, any incriminating evidence remained elusive, hidden in the shadows like the killer himself.

"Artemis," Forester said, his voice low and urgent. "We need to wrap this up soon. We've been in here too long."

"Understood," she replied, her fingers flying over the keys one last time, hoping against hope to find some piece of information that could change the course of their investigation. But as the seconds slipped away, it became increasingly clear that their mission had reached a dead end—leaving them with more questions than answers and a dangerous game far from over.

As she closed the computer and carefully wiped any trace of their presence from the keyboard, she couldn't help but feel a sense of disappointment. They had risked everything to break into this mansion, and now they were leaving empty-handed.

"Let's go," she murmured, following Forester as they crept silently through the darkness, retracing their steps back toward the mansion's entrance. She wanted to check the garage for a woman's bike.

"Wait," Forester suddenly whispered, his hand gripping Artemis's arm in a vice-like hold. "Did you hear that?"

"Probably just the wind," Artemis reassured herself, more than him. But deep down, she knew it wasn't the wind. Something was off, and it set her teeth on edge.

"Artemis!" Forester hissed sharply as they reached the foyer.

In an instant, the darkness was gone, replaced by the harsh glare of overhead lights that flooded the room and left them blinking, momentarily blinded. Artemis squinted through the brightness, her heart pounding in her chest as she saw Giroud standing before them, his eyes cold and unyielding.

"Che cosa state facendo?" he demanded, his Italian dripping with menace.

CHAPTER 15

"Mr. Giroud," she began hesitantly, her mind racing as she crafted a lie on the spot, momentarily floundering to find the words in Italian. "We came here—"

"Save it," Giroud snapped, cutting her off. "I know why you're here. Riccardo sent you, no?"

His icy stare bore into them, leaving them feeling exposed and vulnerable.

"Look, we—" Forester started, but Artemis silenced him with a discreet nudge.

"Mr. Giroud, we apologize for the intrusion," she said, trying to keep her voice steady. "We're not with the mob."

For a moment, Giroud looked puzzled, his furious eyes cut with layers of suspicion. "English?" he said, his voice carrying the lean of his native tongue as he switched languages and guessed at Artemis and Forester's accent.

"Yes," Artemis said hurriedly, feeling a moment of hope rise in her chest as she repeated in English that they were not with the mob.

Giroud regarded them for a moment, his expression inscrutable. Artemis could practically feel the weight of his gaze as he evaluated their sincerity—and decided their fate. The room hummed with the same energy as a hunter's trap about to snap closed, a fragile silence punctuated only by their shallow breaths and the pounding of their hearts.

Giroud's grip tightened around the sleek phone, his thumb hovering over the screen, poised to dial. The bathrobe he wore did little to diminish the imposing figure he cut, standing tall and rigid in the dimly lit hallway.

"Mr. Giroud, please," Artemis pleaded, her voice strained but measured, "we're leaving now. There's no need to involve the authorities."

"Isn't there?" Giroud sneered, the venom in his voice sending a shiver down Forester's spine. "You break into my home, invade my privacy, and expect me to let you walk away without consequence? I know Riccardo sent you. Police are already on their way."

Forester glanced at Artemis, a small tilt of his head and posture silently suggesting he could simply knock out the politician. Shooting back a wide-eyed glance, Artemis made a hurried gesture at her waist, hoping against hope to get out with no one hurt.

But as tension in the room mounted, she knew one thing for sure. She and Forester could not wait around to be arrested.

CHAPTER 16

As THE SLEEK BLACK car followed the serpentine path, anticipation sizzled in the air, an electric undercurrent that crackled with intensity. The winding Italian roads carved their way through the lush countryside, the moon shining down like some distant lighthouse. Ancient vineyards and olive groves adorned the landscape, their gnarled roots telling tales of a bygone era. A balmy breeze rustled the vibrant foliage, carrying with it the scent of rich earth and ripening fruit.

"Turn left at the fork up ahead," said the trembling old man, the humming engine nearly swallowing his words.

"Relax, we'll get there soon enough," replied Leo, the young man behind the wheel. His eyes were focused on the road, seemingly unperturbed by the dangerous game they were playing.

The contrast between the two men was striking, like fire and ice locked together in a precarious dance.

"Please, I don't know how much more I can take," the old man pleaded, his hands shaking as he wrung them together.

"Patience, my friend," Leo murmured, a faint smile playing on his lips. "We have a job to do."

As the car rounded another bend, the old man couldn't help but glance nervously at Leo. Every line of his chiseled face exuded confidence and control, while the old man's own visage was a study in terror.

"Almost there," Leo announced, his tone deceptively casual as they approached the final stretch of road. "Just a bit further." The old man could only nod, his throat dry with fear, as he watched the scenery flash by.

"Remember," Leo continued.

As the sleek black car rounded another treacherously tight bend, Leo couldn't help but admire the way the tires gripped the ancient cobblestones of the winding Italian road. A thrill surged through him as he felt the powerful engine purring beneath his hands. He was a predator on the hunt, and he reveled in it.

"Take the next left," the old man beside him whispered, his voice cracked with fear. He kept his gaze low, avoiding eye contact with Leo at all costs. It was clear that the old man knew he was nothing more than a pawn in this deadly game, and Leo found a certain satisfaction in the power he held over him. He was a master of manipulation, after all, and he'd been honing his skills for years.

The old man had once been called "uncle." But the blood of covenant was thicker than the water of the womb. This man. . . this old, decrepit tomb of a human was nothing more than a nuisance. A means to an end, a fount of information.

He'd been involved with a life of crime once upon a time. . . And he'd caused his share of pain.

"Are you certain?" Leo asked, his voice dripping with condescension. "I wouldn't want to waste any more time retracing our steps."

"Y-yes," stammered the old man, his eyes darting nervously between the road and the imposing figure beside him. "The mansion is just down that road, I swear."

As Leo took the indicated turn, he allowed himself a brief moment of triumph. He had tracked down his prey, meticulously following every breadcrumb until he found himself here, mere moments away from his target. Riccardo, an aging mobster—the last of his breed.

The four horsemen they'd called themselves. Three of them had already been put down. Now for the fourth . . .

His eyes narrowed, and a flash of rage nearly penetrated his attempt at a calm exterior, but he pushed aside the feeling quickly enough.

"Very well," Leo said, his tone ice-cold as he expertly navigated the narrow lane leading toward Riccardo's mansion. "You've proven yourself useful, for now."

The words dangled between them, an unspoken threat that the old man could do little but acknowledge with a meek nod.

The mansion loomed before them, a sinister edifice of brick and stone, partially obscured by the darkness. The iron gates stood sentinel at its entrance, an unwelcoming boundary between the outside world and the dark secrets that lay within. As Leo slowed the car to a stop just short of the gate, he couldn't help but feel a shiver of excitement run down his spine.

"Quite a fortress," Leo remarked, his eyes scanning the perimeter with a calculating precision. Armed guards patrolled the grounds, their steps measured and deliberate, while others monitored security cameras from discreetly placed control rooms. This was no ordinary residence; it was a heavily guarded compound designed to keep unwanted visitors at bay.

"Riccardo certainly doesn't take chances, does he?" Leo mused aloud, drawing a fearful glance from the old man beside him. "But then again, neither do I."

"Wh-what are you going to do?" the old man stuttered, beads of sweat forming on his brow as he nervously shifted in his seat.

"Simple," Leo replied, a wicked smile playing upon his lips. "I'm going to find a way in." He reached into the glove compartment of the car, extracting a pair of binoculars, which he then raised to his eyes.

He studied the mansion's defenses carefully, noting each guard's position, the locations of the security cameras, and any potential weak points in the perimeter. It was a game, one Leo had played many times before, and one he always won. Riccardo's fortress would be no different.

"Ah, there he is," Leo murmured, his gaze fixed upon a towering figure patrolling the front courtyard. Enzo, the formidable giant of a man who had once been a part of Leo's past, now stood as yet another obstacle, a human monolith guarding the entrance to Riccardo's domain. Leo recognized him instantly, the cruel glint in his eyes and the scar that marred his otherwise chiseled features.

"Who?" the old man whispered, craning his neck to catch a glimpse of the figure that had captured Leo's attention.

Leo ignored the question. Instead, he glanced at the old man.

"Thank you," Leo said, his voice soft and melodic as he turned to the man sitting beside him. The old man looked up, startled by the sudden warmth in Leo's tone, his eyes wide with fear and confusion.

"Y-you're welcome," the old man stammered, his voice barely a whisper as he forced a weak smile.

"Ah, no," Leo said, shaking his head gently. "I should be thanking you for bringing me here. I know it was hard for you." He leaned closer to the old man, his breath warm on the old man's cheek. "And I do love a challenge."

With that, Leo placed a tender kiss on the trembling man's cheek. But as their eyes met once more, the old man saw a chilling ruthlessness flicker across Leo's handsome features.

"Wh-what are you going to do now?" the old man asked, his voice quavering as he tried to keep his composure.

"Simple. I'm going to win," Leo replied, his voice cold and unforgiving. And before the old man could process what was happening, Leo pulled out a silenced pistol from his jacket pocket and fired a single shot into the old man's temple.

His body slumped, lifeless, against the car door, his eyes still wide with shock and terror. Leo stared at the corpse for a moment, feeling nothing but satisfaction at having eliminated yet another obstacle in his path. The fact that the old man had served his purpose meant nothing; he was just another pawn in Leo's deadly game.

As the echoes of the silenced gunshot faded into the night, Leo touched the trace of blood on his cheek; his fingers came away red, a vivid contrast to his pale skin and cold expression. In his mind, the old man's life had been forfeited from the moment they had met. And now, with the final piece of the puzzle in place, it was time for Leo to make his move.

"Always so messy," Leo muttered to himself as he wiped the blood from his cheek with a handkerchief. He crumpled the crimson-stained cloth and tossed it onto the corpse. It was time to move forward.

Riccardo won't know what hit him, he thought, a sinister smile creeping across his face. The thrill of the chase had always been irresistible for Leo—the moment when the prey realized they'd been outmaneuvered, the mixture of fear and panic in their eyes. It was intoxicating.

Leo pulled out his phone, scrolling through his contacts until he found the name he was looking for. He pressed the call button and waited for the other person to pick up.

"It's me," he said coolly, his voice betraying no emotion. "I've located Riccardo. Yes . . . yes, I'm sure. Now. Mhmm. Here, I'm sending you the address."

Then, he lowered the phone, and with the dead man still in the seat at his side, he turned the car around and began to move back down the winding road.

It was his job to find them. His job to introduce them to the reaper. And then?

Then came the best part.

CHAPTER 17

ARTEMIS FACED THE SILVER-HAIRED politician as he gripped his phone like a weapon. Giroud eyed them both, his gaze carrying that same steely determination she'd seen in the video where he'd vowed to bring down the four horsemen. Now, though, the ire was directed at her, and there was nowhere to hide. He waved his phone.

"The police will be here soon," he said.

Artemis held up her palms. "It's not what you think. We're here to clear your name."

It was a stretch, but in a way, it was true.

She pressed on. "Riccardo thinks you're the one who's been killing his friends. That puts you in danger."

Giroud blinked, staring at her. "And you expect me to believe you don't work for Riccardo?"

"No, we don't," Artemis said quickly.

Forester remained at her side, quiet and watchful, but she knew that he was tense, coiled like a spring. And if he needed to, he'd burst into action.

"Riccardo is scared. He thinks you're out to get him, and what do you think he'll do?"

Giroud shook his head. "I gave up on caring what Riccardo does a long time ago," he said.

"He killed your brother," Artemis replied. She knew it was a blunt way to put it, but she needed him talking. For the moment, he was disoriented enough to find two intruders in his home, that he wasn't lashing out.

Not yet.

And he'd emerged with a phone in his hand, not a gun. This told her at least something about the man she was dealing with.

"But we believe you're innocent," she said quickly.

She didn't expound, but the schedule she'd found and the public meetings he'd had gave him a solid alibi. And now, facing him, this didn't seem like a man with a guilty conscience. He'd called the police. And he wasn't backing down.

Artemis doubled down on her instinct. Sometimes, especially in high-stress situations, it was all she had to go on.

She kept her anxiety in check, kept her mismatched eyes fixated on the politician whose night slumber they'd interrupted. Something wasn't right. It didn't add up.

She hesitated, staring at the man, trying to make sense of it. She bit her lip, paused, and said, "Do you know anyone else who'd want to hurt those men?"

Giroud blinked. For a moment, he seemed surprised she was even addressing him. Then, his frown deepened. "This isn't an interview," he snapped. "You break into my house and question me? I don't think so." He shook his head adamantly, his accented English delicate in spite of the anger in his voice.

Artemis took a step forward, her hand outstretched in a calming gesture. "I apologize for the intrusion," she began, her voice softening. "But we need your help. We're trying to find out who's behind the murders of those men. And we think you might be able to help us."

Giroud's eyes narrowed, suspicion etched on his features. "And why would I want to help you?" he asked, his voice laced with venom.

"Because we think you're innocent," Artemis replied, holding his gaze. "And because we believe that whoever's behind this is going after Riccardo next . . . but Riccardo thinks it's you. Which means you're in danger. The best way to clear your name is if you help us. "

Giroud hesitated, his eyes flicking between Artemis and Forester. For a moment, he seemed to be weighing his options.

And then, with a shake of his head, he said, "Why should I care if Riccardo dies? In fact, I'd be happy to see it happen." He shrugged. "He killed so many people; not just my brother. He got away with it for long enough. Maybe this is just divine retribution."

Suddenly, in the distance, Artemis spotted flashing red lights through the mirror. The cops were approaching, sirens off.

"He left my brother's wife a widow. His two children fatherless. He ruined more than just one life when he shot my brother." Giroud snorted now. "So no, I don't think I'll be answering any of your questions."

Forester was tugging at Artemis's arm, trying to pull her toward the door. "We need to move," he whispered.

But she felt as if they were so close to finding answers. She stared at Giroud, bit her tongue, then with a sigh turned sharply and began moving toward the door.

"You won't get far!" Giroud warned them. "Tell whoever sent you, next time I'll greet them with a bullet!"

Artemis and Forester didn't stop to exchange words. Once they were out of the house, they broke into a run, heading toward the car they had parked a few streets away. Artemis's heart was pounding, and she could hear the sound of the approaching police cars getting louder. She knew they had to get out of there fast before they were caught.

As they reached the car, Artemis pulled out her phone and dialed a number. Her sister answered a second later as Artemis slipped into the front seat. Forester began to drive.

"Art?" Helen said, her voice full of concern. "Are you okay?"

"Yeah! Yeah, I'm OK," Artemis replied quickly. "How are you? How's Dad, Tommy?"

"Fine. We're all fine. Where's Cameron?"

"He's with me," she said.

Forester cursed as he veered down a side street, shooting quick looks over his shoulder and watching as the dark shapes of police cars veered onto their same street. Had they been spotted? The tires screeched as Cameron moved off on a road between overarching trees.

"When are you coming back?" Helen said, her voice insistent.

"Soon. Very soon."

"And then what, Art?" Helen whispered, her voice strained. "We can't live like this. You can't." She trailed off. "And I know it's all my fault."

"No!" Artemis said sharply. "You can't blame yourself. This isn't your fault."

A long sigh. "What if . . . what if I turn myself in?"

Artemis nearly shouted at this. "No! Helen, listen to me. You're not to blame. Don't. Please, I'm begging you. It would ruin all of us. We need you, Helen. You're the glue that holds our family together. We need you!" She spoke with such urgency that she practically shook.

Helen sighed. "I hate putting you through all of this."

"This time it was Tommy," Artemis shot back. "And the feds are after Dad. And me, now. It's not on you, Helen."

Forester veered down another side street. And now, the rearview mirror was empty.

Artemis stifled a yawn. "I . . . What would you do," she said slowly, equally trying to change the subject, but also trying to get her sister's help, "if someone killed Tommy?"

"Excuse me?"

"It's not wish fulfillment. Promise," Artemis said sardonically. "Just humor me."

"I . . . I don't know."

"Let's say someone did it and Tommy was just an innocent victim. How would you react? How would most people react?"

"I'd . . . want justice, I guess."

Artemis sighed, nodding. "But what if the person who'd want justice has an alibi."

"Maybe they hired someone."

Artemis paused. "I don't think so. No record of it. No transactions I saw . . . and he wasn't a guilty man. The cops were his lifeline. No . . ."

"Then . . . who else stands to benefit from the death of my brother's murderer," Helen said quietly. "Maybe it's a power play. Maybe someone's just using the veneer of vengeance to get what they really want."

Artemis frowned, considering these words.

But she was too tired and could feel her head nodding. Mentally exhausted, though her body was still racing with adrenaline as they sped down the dark streets.

"Motel about five minutes from here," Forester said, glancing at her. "Stop?"

She considered this but then nodded. A place to rest. To sleep. And then, under the cover of morning . . . perhaps they'd see things more clearly.

She shot Forester a sidelong glance, and he gave her a look. "How's Helen?"

Artemis bid her sister farewell, lowered the phone, and then just said, "Holding on. She said they're fine. Everyone's safe."

Inwardly, she wasn't sure if this was true at all. She wasn't sure if they'd ever be fine again. But she refused to resign herself to this line of thinking. All she could do was try and protect everyone.

But in order to do that, she had to clear Tommy. She had to find the serial killer targeting mobsters. And she had the distinct impression she was running out of time.

CHAPTER 18

THE MOTEL ROOM WAS dimly lit, the pale glow of a single flickering light bulb casting shadows on the peeling wallpaper. The air felt heavy with age and neglect, only serving to amplify the weight pressing down on Artemis's chest as she lay in bed, tossing and turning. Her coal black hair fanned out around her, sticking to her damp forehead as the sweat beaded along her skin.

"Damn it," she muttered under her breath, clenching her fists beneath the threadbare sheets. Sleep had eluded her for hours now, leaving her trapped in her own thoughts—an unwelcome and disquieting place to be at a time like this. In moments like these, when the darkness seemed to swallow her whole, her mind raced with strategies and contingencies, calculating moves and countermoves like pieces on a chessboard. But tonight, the game was one she could not win.

Finally relenting to her restlessness and throwing aside the thin covers, she swung her legs over the side of the bed and planted her feet firmly on the cold tile floor.

As she rose from the bed, she glanced at herself in the cracked mirror above the dresser. Her pretty features were sallow and drawn, with dark circles underlining her eyes. A bitter smile played on her lips as she briefly considered how far she had come, and yet how little had changed.

She padded softly across the room to the door, her bare feet making no sound on the cold tiles. Pausing for a moment, she took a deep breath, attempting to steady her racing heart. "It's just Forester," she reminded herself. "He'll understand."

The night had draped itself over the Italian countryside, casting a thick blanket of darkness pierced only by scattered pinpricks of starlight. Forester stood on the small balcony attached to his motel room, his tall frame silhouetted against the celestial backdrop. His disheveled hair rustled in the gentle breeze, while the scent of olive groves and cypress trees wafted up from the valley below.

He was still awake, just like Artemis. Sleep hadn't come easy for either of them since they'd gone on the run, but tonight seemed particularly cruel. Forester's cast-encased arm hung heavily at his side, a constant reminder of their vulnerability. He knew that being able to rest meant letting his guard down, something he couldn't afford. For now, however, he allowed himself the luxury of gazing out into the peaceful landscape beyond.

"Maybe it won't always be like this," he mused, trying to imagine a life where they could escape the relentless pursuit of their enemies, a life where they wouldn't have to keep looking over their shoulders.

His thoughts were interrupted by a soft knock on the door. Forester tensed, his instincts sharpened by months of living on the edge. He carefully stepped back inside the room, leaving the balcony doors ajar. The ambiance shifted as the world outside faded slightly, replaced by the dim light of the small bedside lamp he'd left on.

"Who is it?" he called out cautiously, his voice low and gravelly.

"Forester, it's me," came the hushed reply, urgency threading through her tone. "I can't sleep. Can I come in?"

Relief washed over him, quickly followed by concern. He knew how strong-willed Artemis was, and for her to seek solace meant she was truly struggling. Despite their situation, a small part of him felt a swell of pride that she trusted him enough to let her guard down around him.

"Of course," he said, opening the door. His eyes met hers, and he could see the shape of desperation lurking beneath her otherwise stoic demeanor.

"Thank you," Artemis murmured as she stepped inside, closing the door behind her with a soft click. Her gaze drifted to the balcony, where the Italian countryside stretched out like a painting, its tranquility at odds with the turmoil in her mind.

"Forester, I . . . I just can't seem to quiet my thoughts tonight," she admitted, her voice barely more than a whisper. "I thought maybe being near you would help."

Forester's tired, caring eyes met Artemis's as he wordlessly stepped aside, inviting her into his room. She crossed the threshold and instantly felt a sense of warmth and safety that had been absent from her own space.

"Thank you," she whispered, her voice nearly indistinct, as she moved past him toward the open balcony doors. The moonlit Italian countryside stretched out before her eyes, a stunning panorama of rolling hills, vineyards, and ancient villas nestled in the darkness.

"Beautiful, isn't it?" Forester asked, following her gaze. His voice was low and soothing, like the distant hum of a cello. Artemis nodded, unable to tear her eyes away from the mesmerizing view.

"Sometimes I forget how much beauty there is in the world," she said softly, her loose bedclothes rippling in the gentle night breeze. "Especially when we're constantly on the run."

Forester joined her at the edge of the balcony, allowing a moment of silence to pass between them. "I know," he finally said, reaching for her hand and giving it a reassuring squeeze. "But that's why we have each other, right? To remind ourselves that there's still something worth fighting for."

Artemis turned to face him, her pretty features illuminated by the silvery light of the moon. "I couldn't do this without you, Forester."

"Same here, Checkers," he admitted. "You make me want to be a better man."

As the wind rustled through the trees below, Artemis allowed herself to lean into Forester's embrace, feeling a surge of calm wash over her.

Forester's right arm, encased in a cast from wrist to elbow, rested awkwardly against his body. The stark-white plaster stood out against the darkness of the night. Despite the injury, he managed to exude an air of strength and determination.

"Does it still hurt?" she asked quietly, her gaze drawn to the cast as they stood side by side on the balcony.

"Only when I forget it's there," Forester admitted with a wry smile. "But the pain's nothing compared to what we've been through."

Artemis moved closer to him, their shoulders touching as she leaned into his warmth. She felt the steady rhythm of his heartbeat beneath the worn fabric of his shirt and the brush of his disheveled hair against her forehead as he tilted his head slightly to accommodate her.

"Thank you," she whispered, her voice as faint as the distant rustle of leaves below them. "For being here."

Forester turned his head to look at her, his scarred palm reaching up to gently brush a strand of midnight black hair away from her face.

Artemis hesitated for a moment, her hand hovering just above the curve of Forester's back. She could feel the warmth emanating from him even through the layers of clothing that separated them. With a gentle touch, she began to massage his back, careful not to jar his injured arm.

"Are you okay?" she asked softly, her fingers working out the tension that had settled into the muscles beneath his shoulder blades.

Forester sighed, the sound a mixture of relief and appreciation. "Yeah," he replied, his voice low and gravelly, like the distant rumble of thunder as they slipped into quiet together. "Promise me something, Artemis," Forester said suddenly, breaking the silence that had settled between them. "Promise me that no matter what happens, we'll never lose this. This connection."

"Forester . . ." The weight of his request made her breath catch, but Artemis didn't hesitate. She knew that whatever challenges lay ahead, they would be infinitely more bearable with him by her side. "I promise."

As if sensing her unspoken resolve, Forester wrapped his good arm around her, pulling her close to his chest. The strength of his embrace was both surprising and reassuring as if he were silently vowing to shield her from the evils that threatened to encroach upon their fragile sanctuary.

"Let's get some sleep," he suggested, his breath warm against her ear. "We've got a long day ahead of us."

"Right," Artemis agreed, extracting herself from his grip with some reluctance. As they turned to leave the balcony, she couldn't help but feel a renewed sense of hope and purpose. They might be on the run, pursued by an unseen enemy and haunted by their own demons, but in this moment, Artemis knew that she was exactly where she needed to be. And as they stepped back into the dimly lit motel room, leaving the moon-lit countryside behind them, she couldn't help but think that maybe, just maybe, everything would be alright after all.

CHAPTER 19

ARTEMIS SAT AT THE small table in the motel, her eyes bleary as she stared at the computer. She was watching the video of Giroud again . . . and again . . . and again. She frowned as she hit replay once more.

Something in the frame caught her attention. Something Helen had said was now roused by the sunlight streaming over the Italian countryside and through her window.

Who else could be involved?

She shivered.

Something else . . . something Giroud had said. The four horse-men had left a woman a widow . . . and two children fatherless.

One of the children happened to be in the video with his father. An aide. Standing in the back. Now, she recognized him.

Leo Giroud.

And as his father spoke, Leo stood in the back with a stoic expression. Except for one moment. The moment when his father started yelling, vowing vengeance on the mobsters. And in that moment, Leo's expression had morphed. Something sinister had emerged under the features. Something almost ghoulish.

She sat hunched over in the small motel room, fingers drumming rhythmically on the cheap desk as her mind raced with precision. Artemis knew that time was running out; she needed a plan and fast.

"Forester," she whispered, trying to keep her voice steady despite the urgency bubbling inside her. "Forester, wake up."

In the bed behind her, the tall, scarred man stirred beneath the thin motel sheets. His disheveled hair lay plastered to his forehead as he blinked open his eyes. He propped himself up on one elbow, groggily rubbing his face with the other hand.

"Artemis?" Forester grumbled, his voice thick with sleep. "What's wrong?"

"Nothing's wrong," she replied, attempting to inject some levity into her tone but failing miserably. "I just need your help with something."

Forester sighed, swinging his legs out from under the covers and onto the cold linoleum floor.

"Alright," he said, pulling on his rumpled shirt and joining her at the desk. "What do you need me to do?"

"Convince Desmond Wade to help us with the investigation," Artemis said without hesitation, her eyes never leaving the computer screen. "We're so close, Forester. I can feel it. We just need to access security footage of the intersections near the 'mobsters' houses.' "

"Footage?"

"Bike paths that intersect roads," she said, nodding firmly. She winced. "Can you do that?"

"Are you sure about this?" Forester asked, concern etched in his furrowed brow. "Wade's not exactly . . . on our team anymore."

"Desperate times call for desperate measures," Artemis replied quietly, her fingers now still on the desk as she turned to face him.

Forester hesitated for a moment longer, searching her eyes for any sign of hesitation.

"Alright," he finally agreed, reaching for his phone. "I'll do it. But I can't promise anything."

"Thank you," Artemis breathed, her shoulders visibly relaxing as Forester began to dial Wade's number.

The phone rang for what felt like too long. Artemis studied Forester's face carefully.

"Where are you two?" Wade's curt voice crackled through the speaker almost as soon as the connection was made. There was no pretense of pleasantries, no attempt at civility. Just a blunt demand for information.

"Never mind that," Forester replied, his voice steady despite the unease that gnawed at his gut. "We need your help, Wade."

"Huh. Nah."

"Nah?"

"Nah."

"Cut the crap, Wade," Forester snapped, his scarred hand gripping the phone tightly.

"Hello, Wade," Artemis interjected softly, her voice silken and measured. She leaned forward, resting her elbows on the table. "We're in a bit of a bind here, and we desperately need your help. Specifically, we need access to some Italian security footage."

"Absolutely not," Wade replied curtly, his words clipped and terse. "I don't know what you two think you're doing, but I won't be a part of it. You should come in. Both of you."

"You know we can't do that," Forester countered. "Just a peek at the footage, for old times' sake."

"My hands are tied," Wade retorted, his impatience evident. "I'm not about to risk my career."

Silence filled the small motel room as Forester watched Artemis, her face a mask of stoicism as she processed Wade's refusal.

"Alright, listen, Desmond," Forester interjected, his voice steady and assertive. "We go way back, you and I. We've pulled each other out of some tight spots over the years, haven't we?"

A brief silence followed, punctuated by Wade's reluctant sigh. "Yes, we have," he admitted, his voice betraying a hint of nostalgia amid the frustration.

"Remember that time in Mexico? I'm pretty sure I saved your life, didn't I?" Forester continued, a slight smile playing on his lips as he recalled the memory.

"Saved my life?" Wade scoffed. "You nearly got us both killed! It was me who had to drag you out of that burning building after you tripped the alarm!"

"Ah, but who took out the sniper that had you pinned down in the Keys?" Forester countered.

"Only after I'd taken out three of his buddies and disarmed the bomb!" Wade retorted.

"Yeah? And what about Utah?"

A pause. "You said you'd never mention Utah," Wade countered.

"Yeh, well . . . desperate times, Wade."

A sigh. "Why don't you two just come in? Hmm?"

"And get arrested again?"

"It's not like that."

"I don't want to talk shop, Wade," Forester said. "Are you going to help? You owe me."

"Because of Utah?"

"Because of Utah."

"Fine," Wade grumbled after a moment's silence. "You win, Forester. I'll send you the footage, but don't expect me to keep bailing you out of trouble."

"Thank you, Desmond," Artemis said, her voice softening with gratitude. "We appreciate your help."

"Right," Wade replied curtly. "Text me the details. I'll get the video files to you as soon as possible. Don't get caught." The call ended abruptly, leaving Artemis and Forester in an uneasy quiet.

Artemis glanced at Forester, who was rubbing his scarred palm absentmindedly. "He didn't sound happy about that," she observed, trying to gauge Forester's thoughts on the matter.

"He's not," Forester admitted, staring at his phone for a moment before setting it down. "But he'll come through. He always does."

"Is that what friendship is like in your world?" Artemis asked, half-jokingly. "Saving each other from mortal danger and then arguing about who owes whom?"

"Something like that," Forester answered, a wistful smile spreading across his face. "It keeps life interesting."

Time passed far too slowly for Artemis's liking as she double-checked the intersections nearest the crime scenes.

Eventually, at long last, a soft ping of an email notification cut through the stifling silence like a knife, jolting Artemis and Forester from their anxious reverie. Artemis's heart leaped into her throat as she clicked on the new message, her eyes scanning the subject line: "Security Footage—As Requested."

"Finally," she breathed, her voice barely above a whisper, as she quickly downloaded the attachments and opened the video files.

"Let's hope Wade came through for us," Forester said, his deep voice laced with equal parts hope and apprehension. He moved closer to the computer screen, his scarred palm resting against the back of Artemis's chair.

"Indeed," Artemis murmured, her fingers drumming against the desk in anticipation. As the first video began to play, her sharp, analytical mind switched into high gear, dissecting every pixel of the grainy footage.

Scene by scene, the two of them watched the footage. Neither of them spoke, both engrossed by the video feed.

Cars passed by. Bikes paused. Pedestrians moved across the road. Even a small herd of cattle in one of the videos. Artemis kept the three streams of footage running simultaneously. But nothing emerged.

She clicked her tongue, shaking her head and feeling her frustration mounting.

"Nothing," Forester was saying. He was skipping through large sections of the video now.

"Wait! There!" Artemis shouted as she pointed at the screen. "Rewind that!"

Forester quickly rewound the video to the time stamp she had indicated, and they both leaned in closer, studying the blurry image of an intersection.

"Right there," she said, tapping the screen with a slender finger. "Do you see it?"

"Damn," Forester murmured, his scarred palm resting on the edge of the table.

On the screen, a figure on a bike, clad in a hooded jacket, sped away from the intersection. Despite the spotty angle of the footage, there was something about the way the figure moved—swift and agile. On a woman's bike and steering one-handed. Left-handed.

"Looks like we've got ourselves a lead," Forester said, a hint of relief in his voice. "But how do we track this person?"

Artemis's mind raced, her thoughts whirring like the gears of a well-oiled machine as she considered their options.

Was this Leo Giroud?

She stared at the image, trying to parse some detail or clue from the image. A few seconds passed, and the figure on screen raising his wrist to study a dark band. Artemis froze. "Forester," she whispered.

"What?"

"The watch."

"What about the watch?"

She pointed. "It's a Rolex."

"What? You sure?"

"Look! I recognize it. Leo had the same watch!"

"Giroud's son?"

"Yeah. Look." She cycled back to the news video and pointed out the watch in question. She flashed a quick smile and a nod. "He's our guy, Cameron. He's the killer."

CHAPTER 20

ARTEMIS AND CAMERON PULLED up to the publicly listed address of Leo Giroud, both of them cautious as they pushed from their vehicle and approached the modest door of the equally modest home. Nothing suggested a serial killer might lurk behind those doors.

The early morning sun peeked over the horizon, casting a soft golden glow on the quaint Veneto village. Artemis and Forester stared at the modest home before them, its white stucco walls and terra-cotta roof tiles making it indistinguishable from the others lining the cobblestone street. The air was thick with the scent of freshly baked bread and brewing espresso, but beneath the surface, an eerie tension lingered.

As they approached the door, Artemis couldn't help but feel an uneasy stiffness in her spine. Despite the apparent normalcy of the scene, she knew there was a darkness lurking beneath—one that had led to a string of brutal murders, all tied to their main suspect, Leo Giroud. She recalled the security footage they had painstakingly analyzed, homing in on two key details: first, Leo's left-handedness, which matched the killer's profile; and second, the gleaming Rolex watch on his wrist.

As they reached the door, Artemis took a deep breath and knocked firmly. Her mind raced, trying to predict every possible scenario that might unfold once they came face-to-face with Leo Giroud.

There was no answer to their knock, but the door creaked open slightly under Artemis's insistent hand. Forester looked at her, and she nodded. Stepping inside, they were greeted by a living room that seemed frozen in time—a half-eaten meal on the table, a newspaper sprawled across the couch, and a coffee cup resting on the windowsill. Yet, there was no sign of life.

"Strange," Forester muttered, his voice barely above a whisper as they continued their search. Artemis couldn't help but agree, feeling a cold chill of anticipation gripping her heart. The house seemed eerily empty.

"Check the garage, I'll look upstairs," Artemis directed, her voice steady despite the unease gnawing at her. She could sense

Forester's reluctance to split up, but they both knew it would be faster this way.

"Be careful, Artemis," he warned before moving toward the garage, his scarred hand gripping the door handle tightly.

Ascending the narrow staircase, Artemis's mind raced with thoughts of what she might find, or worse, what she wouldn't find. Each step seemed to shout through the hollow house, amplifying her anxiety. She systematically checked each bedroom, bathroom, and closet, finding nothing more than neatly made beds and folded clothes.

"Empty," she whispered into the small radio clipped to her shirt. "You?"

"Same here," Forester's voice crackled back. "No sign of him."

Artemis frowned, frustrated by the lack of answers. What had happened to Leo Giroud?

Just then, she heard it—the unmistakable sound of tires crunching on gravel outside. She rushed to the window, peering out just in time to see a car pulling into the driveway. Her pulse quickened, adrenaline surging through her veins as she realized their suspect had just arrived.

"Forester," she whispered urgently into the radio. "He's here."

"Got it," he replied, his voice tense with anticipation. "I'm coming."

Without waiting for him, Artemis slipped out of the bedroom and crept down the stairs, her every sense heightened as she moved silently toward the front door. Peeking through the crack, she watched as Leo Giroud emerged from the car, his left hand casually gripping the door handle while the Rolex watch glinted in the morning sunlight.

"Forester, get down," Artemis whispered urgently as she observed Leo's movements.

Cameron had appeared at her side, also peering through the window.

"Shit," Forester muttered under his breath, catching sight of the blood smeared on Leo's face. It was as if a macabre paintbrush had stained his visage with crimson streaks. But it wasn't just the blood that unnerved them; it was the lifeless body slumped in the passenger seat of the car, its head lolling at an unnatural angle.

"Who is that?" Forester asked softly.

As they watched, Leo opened the garage door and disappeared inside, emerging moments later with a large black bag and an ax clutched in his left hand. The gleaming blade caught the morning sunlight, casting its reflection on the gravel driveway. Their suspect's involvement in a violent act was now undeniable.

"Go!" Artemis whispered urgently, her heart pounding in her chest as she and Forester sprang from their cover.

They took the steps two at a time and burst out the front door.

"Police! Get down on the ground!" Forester barked, his weapon drawn and aimed at Leo's chest. Artemis could see the beads of sweat forming on Forester's brow.

The handsome son of the murdered Timothe Giroud froze. He stared at them briefly. His head tilted slowly to the side as if he couldn't be fazed.

"Damn it," Leo muttered under his breath as if sensing the gravity of his situation. For a moment, it seemed as though he would comply with Forester's demand—but then, with a sudden burst of energy, he made his move.

He bolted back toward his car, flinging himself into the front seat. He peeled out of the driveway as Forester shot out the side mirror. But the car was still speeding away.

"Follow him!" Artemis ordered, dashing toward their own vehicle parked nearby. Leo was desperate, and desperation made people unpredictable. She couldn't afford any mistakes now.

They both flung themselves into their own vehicle, moving rapidly.

"Stay with him, Forester!" she urged as they gave chase, her voice a mix of determination and concern.

"Trying my best," he replied tersely, his knuckles white on the steering wheel as they tore down the narrow streets of northern Italy in pursuit of their quarry.

As the car swerved around tight bends and obstacles, Artemis gripped the door handle, feeling the vibrations of the engine beneath her.

"Left, Forester!" Artemis shouted as she spotted Leo's car swerving onto a back road. The early morning light cast long shadows across the narrow lane lined with ancient stone walls and olive trees whose gnarled branches seemed to reach out toward them.

"Copy that," Forester replied, gripping the steering wheel tightly, his scarred palm slick with sweat. The tires screeched as they rounded the corner, their vehicle lurching perilously close to the edge.

Artemis's heart pounded in her chest, her breath coming in short, sharp bursts. She scanned the road ahead. "He's heading for the vineyards," she said, her voice tight with urgency.

"Damn it," muttered Forester, pushing the accelerator down harder. They weaved between the few other cars on the road, their speed leaving the sleepy morning drivers staring after them in bewilderment. The engine roared beneath them, a wild beast straining against its leash.

"Forester, I need you to get us alongside him," Artemis demanded, her mind racing through scenarios. She knew that if they could force Leo off the road, they'd stand a better chance of apprehending him. But how?

"Working on it," he grunted, teeth gritted in concentration. Their car picked up speed, closing the gap between them and Leo.

Finally, they drew level with Leo's car, the two vehicles hurtling down the narrow road like dueling knights in a breakneck joust. Artemis clenched her fists, her knuckles white as she braced for impact.

"NOW!" she screamed, and Forester jerked the wheel toward Leo's vehicle. The cars collided with a sickening crunch, metal buckling under the force. Leo's car veered off course, careening through a flimsy wooden barricade and into a vineyard.

"Follow him!" Artemis ordered, her eyes locked on the plume of dust rising from Leo's path. As their car plunged into the vineyard, they found themselves tearing through rows of grapevines, the plants snapping and crashing against the windshield.

"Where is he?" Forester yelled over the cacophony, his gaze darting between the vines, searching for any sign of their quarry. Artemis strained her eyes, trying to pick out the telltale glint of sunlight reflecting off metal or glass. The vines and branches around them hid their vehicle.

"Up ahead!" Artemis shouted, pointing to where Leo's car had come to an abrupt halt, its wheels buried in the soft earth between two rows of grapevines. The vines tangled around the vehicle's undercarriage, as if trying to hold it captive.

"Damn," Forester muttered, gritting his teeth as he slammed on the brakes, bringing their own vehicle to a screeching halt mere inches from Leo's rear bumper.

Suddenly, the air filled with the roar of an engine as Leo managed to free his car from the grasping vines. He threw the vehicle into reverse, narrowly missing Artemis and Forester's car by mere inches as he sped backward down the row of grapevines.

As they approached a bend in the rows of vines, the sharp staccato of gunfire rang out, the sound bouncing back off the hills surrounding the vineyard. Artemis instinctively ducked, her heart leaping into her throat as she felt the impact of bullets on their car.

"He's shooting at us!" she cried, anger giving her voice an edge. "Forester, get us out of his line of fire!"

"Working on it!" Forester's face was a grim mask as he wrenched the wheel to the side, their vehicle swerving wildly in response.

But it was too late. A bullet found its mark, puncturing their front tire with lethal accuracy. The sound of rushing air and the sudden jolt of the car dipping to one side confirmed their situation—they were now at a severe disadvantage.

"Damn it!" Forester growled, struggling to maintain control as their crippled vehicle shuddered and veered off course. Adrenaline coursed through Artemis as she gripped the door handle, her mind racing to find a way out of this predicament.

With the car's tire punctured and their momentum waning, Forester leaned out of the window, his scarred hand gripping the pistol with practiced ease. He focused on the fleeing vehicle, tracking its movements carefully before taking two well-placed shots. The sound of gunfire was deafening in the confined space, but it seemed to do the trick—Leo's back tires exploded in a spray of rubber and smoke, forcing his car to screech to an abrupt stop.

"Got him!" Forester exclaimed, satisfaction evident in his voice.

"Good work," Artemis praised, her relief palpable. But there was no time to celebrate; they needed to apprehend Leo before he could make another move.

As they sprinted toward Leo's vehicle, Artemis's mind teemed with questions and possibilities. What would they find when they reached him? Would he surrender willingly, or would their pursuit end in bloodshed? The uncertainty gnawed at her, but she pushed it aside.

The stench of burned rubber and twisted metal assaulted Artemis's senses as she and Forester raced toward Leo's car, their bodies slick with sweat and hearts pounding like drums. The adrenaline coursing through her veins felt like fire, sharpening her focus to a razor's edge. She could almost taste the fear in the air—it was thick, heavy, and suffocating.

"Stay close," Forester instructed between labored breaths, his gravelly voice betraying the strain of their pursuit. "We don't know what he's planning."

"Right behind you," Artemis assured him, her dark locks whipping against her flushed cheeks as they closed in on their target.

They reached the mangled wreckage of Leo's vehicle, its once-pristine exterior now marred by jagged tears and shattered glass. Artemis surveyed the scene, her keen mind absorbing every detail—the way the vines coiled around the twisted metal like angry snakes, the faint scent of gasoline that hung in the air, the eerie silence that seemed to swallow them whole.

"See anything?" Forester asked, his eyes scanning the area for any sign of movement.

"Nothing yet," Artemis replied, her gaze lingering on the bloodied passenger seat and the chilling sight of the ax and large bag strewn haphazardly on the ground. "But he can't have gone far."

"Keep your guard up," Forester warned, his grip tightening on his weapon. "He could be hiding nearby."

As if on cue, a rustle in the underbrush caught their attention, followed by the unmistakable sound of footsteps crunching on gravel. Artemis's heart leaped into her throat, her instincts screaming at her that the moment of truth was upon them.

"Leo Giroud!" Forester bellowed, his authoritative voice cutting through the dense silence. "Show yourself! It's over!"

Artemis tensed, every muscle in her body coiled and ready to spring into action. She knew that the next few moments could mean the difference between life and death, and she refused to be caught off guard.

"Forester, I think he's—" she began, but her words were abruptly cut off by a deafening blast that rolled through the vineyard like thunder.

A gunshot.

"Get down!" Forester yelled, pushing Artemis to the ground. Her heart hammered against her rib cage, the taste of fear bitter on her tongue as she scrambled for cover.

After a second, the sounds faded.

"Let's go," she urged, unable to hear her own words against the ringing in her ears. Together, they crept forward, inching closer and closer to the source of the gunshot, their fates hanging in the balance.

As they rounded the final bend, another shot rang out, its bark sending shivers down Artemis's spine. This time, however, there was no accompanying hail of bullets—only an eerie silence that seemed to stretch on for an eternity.

"Forester?" Artemis whispered, her voice trembling with uncertainty. "What just happened?"

"Stay back," he warned, his eyes narrowing as he peered into the darkness.

Artemis held her breath, straining to hear any sign of movement or life amid the oppressive silence. The air was thick with tension, a palpable force that seemed to press down upon them like a heavy weight.

Artemis slowly emerged, peering toward the rear of the parked vehicle. Leo Giroud had attempted to sneak back to his car.

Artemis's breath caught in her throat as she and Forester stumbled to a halt by Leo's car, their eyes widening in shock at the scene before them. The door hung open, and there, sprawled on the ground amid the crushed grapes and churned-up earth, lay Leo Giroud, his lifeless body a testament to the finality of the gunshot they had just heard.

"Shit," Forester whispered hoarsely, unable to tear his gaze away from the grisly sight. Artemis felt her stomach roil, bile rising at the back of her throat, but she swallowed it down, forcing herself to remain focused even as her mind reeled from the sudden turn of events.

"Is he . . .?" she managed to choke out, her voice only just audible over the pounding of her own heart.

"Dead," Forester confirmed grimly, his scarred hand clenching into a tight fist at his side. "He must have shot himself."

Artemis stared down at Leo's body, her dark eyes searching for any signs of movement, any hint that this might be another one of his twisted games. But there was none, only the stillness of death and the stench of blood mingling with the scent of crushed grapes and damp earth. She shivered involuntarily, wrapping her arms around herself as if to ward off the chill that settled in her bones.

"I guess . . . I guess that means . . ." she trailed off, uncertain what to say.

She swallowed, shaking her head and looking away. The corpse of the old man was still in the front passenger seat. So much death.

She shivered, and then she turned away, her hands shaking. She didn't want Forester to see her trembling fingers. As Forester kicked the gun away from Leo's body, she pulled out her phone. She inhaled shakily, then exhaled again.

She couldn't help Leo's victims. Couldn't help his father, who'd been killed by the mob. Couldn't help Leo himself . . .

But her brother? Her sister and father?

She pressed the phone against her cheek as it rang, dialing the number Tommy had provided her after the shoot-out in their Venetian hotel. Two rings.

"What?" snapped the voice.

"I found the man who's been hunting your friends," she said quietly.

The voice on the other end paused. The uncle of the man who'd been in the car Tommy had been driving. Another criminal, another killer. She was growing tired of these people.

"You found him?"

"He's dead," she said simply.

Another long pause. Then a sneer. "How stupid do you think I am?"

"No. I'm serious."

"I'm serious!" the voice bellowed.

"I'm staring at his corpse right now," she insisted.

"Yeah? Hmm? If that's so, why the hell was Matteo Riccardo just kidnapped from his own home? Huh?"

"Wait, what?"

"Happened fifteen minutes ago. I just got the damn call, bitch."

Artemis stared at the phone. What sort of game was he playing? But he didn't sound like he was playing a game. It sounded like he thought he was telling the truth.

"How's . . . how's that possible?" she murmured more to herself than to the mobster on the phone.

"Maybe because you didn't do your job properly," the voice on the other end spat. "Or maybe because you're in cahoots with the bastard."

Artemis clenched her jaw, her fingers white-knuckled around the phone. "I did my job," she growled. "And I'm not in cahoots with anyone. I found the man who did this, and he's dead. I swear it."

There was a long silence on the other end of the line, and Artemis held her breath, waiting for a response. After what felt like an eternity, the voice spoke again, its tone low and dangerous.

"I don't play games, Blythe. Your brother is gonna swing."

And then the line went dead.

Forester was watching her, frowning. "Everything okay?" he asked.

"No," she said, blinking in the morning sun. "No, it's not. Not at all."

CHAPTER 21

THEY STOOD ON A hill, amid the wooded lot, watching the scene in the distance.

"Quite a scene, isn't it?" Artemis murmured, her eyes locked on the sprawling mansion surrounded by an imposing wrought iron fence. The grand building loomed in the distance, but what captured her attention were the swarms of police officers who moved about like ants in a frenzy of activity.

"Mhmm," Forester replied gruffly, the scar on his palm itching as he clenched his fist, a telltale sign that danger was near.

Sirens wailed, their shrill cry slicing through the air, adding to the cacophony of chaos. Flashing blue and red lights bounced off the mansion's opulent walls, strobing madly across the manicured lawns. The urgency of the situation was palpable, the air thick with tension.

Officers armed with rifles dashed around the perimeter, their faces taut with concentration, while others barked orders into radios. The occasional snap of branches from the nearby woods only served to heighten the atmosphere of unease.

Artemis crouched low, her dark clothing and hair melding seamlessly with the shadows as she observed the unfolding commotion through narrowed eyes. The once-exclusive mansion had transformed into a frenetic tableau of flashing lights and agitated law enforcement. Her mind, always calculating, processed each detail methodically; she noted the patterns of the officers' movements, the distribution of their force.

"Looks like they've got every available resource on this," Forester whispered beside her, crouching low himself.

"Indeed," Artemis agreed, distantly. "The caller was right; someone's taken Matteo."

"Damn," Forester muttered, running a hand through his hair. "This just got a lot more complicated."

Neither of them could forget Leo Giroud—his body would soon be discovered by the police they had called back to their own position. But Leo clearly hadn't been working alone.

"Complicated, yes, but not insurmountable." Artemis's gaze never wavered from the scene before her. "We need to gather as much information as possible while we still have the element of surprise. Look for anything out of place—anyone who might be involved in the kidnapping."

"Got it." Forester's expression hardened, determination etched across his face. "Look," he added, nodding. "See anything familiar?"

Artemis hesitated but then realized what he meant. Matteo's familiar bodyguard was also on scene.

Enzo, the human mountain that he was, moved away from the sea of uniformed officers and yellow crime scene tape. Artemis observed his hulking figure carefully as he fumbled in his pockets for a cigarette and lighter. The flicker of a flame illuminated his stern features as he lit the tobacco, inhaled deeply, then exhaled a plume of smoke into the night sky.

"Forester," Artemis breathed as if afraid she might be heard over the distant hum of police radios and crime scene chatter, "he's alone."

Forester's gaze locked on Enzo as well. His scarred hand tightened around a sturdy branch. "We need answers," he muttered, as if giving an excuse.

"I know . . . but . . ." she trailed off.

Artemis nodded, her heart racing with adrenaline. She knew their timing had to be perfect; one misstep could lead to disaster.

"Get ready," she told Forester, who nodded in response and slipped behind a nearby tree, hidden from view but close enough to strike if needed.

Taking a deep breath to steady her nerves, Artemis lifted her fingers to her lips and let out a sharp whistle that pierced through the air like a bullet. Enzo's head snapped toward the sound, his eyes scanning the dark tree line as he tried to pinpoint the source.

"Over here," Artemis called out, stepping from behind a tree, making herself visible but staying just out of reach. Her hands were empty and held out at her sides, showing she posed no immediate threat.

Enzo took a step forward, towering over her like a storm cloud. The giant's eyes narrowed, a flash of recognition lighting up his gaze as he focused on Artemis. "You!" he spat, fury radiating from him like heat from a furnace. His enormous hands clenched into fists the size of sledgehammers, and his chest heaved with barely controlled rage.

"Surprised to see me?" Artemis asked, hoping to buy Forester some time. The longer she could keep Enzo focused on her . . .

"Should've known you'd show up eventually," Enzo growled. Artemis didn't have to understand every word to pick up the Italian giant's meaning as he took another step toward her. "You were involved. I told him! Where is he? What'd you do to him!" Enzo growled now, fingers flexing as he reached toward Artemis.

As if on cue, Forester burst from the underbrush behind Enzo, his face a mask of determination as he swung a thick branch at the hulking man's head with all his might. The sound of wood meeting flesh reverberated through the forest, and Enzo staggered forward, momentarily stunned by the blow.

Enzo's massive frame quivered, his face contorted with rage and pain. To Artemis's astonishment, he was still standing, barely affected by the crushing blow Forester had delivered.

Forester briefly glanced at the branch, shrugged, and swung again. The branch whistled through the air, connecting with a sickening thud against Enzo's temple. Enzo's knees buckled beneath him. The bodyguard crumpled to the ground like a felled oak, finally unconscious.

Forester breathed heavily as he surveyed the damage. "We need to move fast. No telling how long he'll be out."

"Right," Artemis agreed, her mind already racing with plans and contingencies. What secrets did Enzo hold locked away in that oversized skull of his? She was about to find out, one way or another.

CHAPTER 22

ARTEMIS WAS ONCE AGAIN glad to have Forester's resourcefulness; without him, they never would've found a quiet, secluded location. But he'd used the GPS to find a nearby storage shed.

The air inside the small wooden shack was thick with tension, its seclusion only amplifying the unease that weighed heavily on the atmosphere. The sunbeams that managed to penetrate the gaps between the planks cast irregular bars of light on the faces of Forester and Artemis, who stood side by side, their expressions a mix of determination and trepidation.

Artemis brushed a strand of her hair behind her ear, her pretty features softening as she observed Enzo's futile attempts to break free from his restraints. Like a chess master surveying the board before making her move, she watched Enzo keenly, taking note of every detail.

Enzo's physical appearance, on the other hand, was one of brute strength. His massive frame strained against the ropes that bound him to the chair, muscles bulging with each effort. Sweat trickled down his temples, highlighting the prominent veins on his forehead. Every movement he made seemed to showcase his raw power, like a caged animal desperate for freedom.

"Enzo," Forester said, his deep voice cutting through the silence, "we're not here to hurt you." The tall man moved closer, his messy hair casting an eerie shadow over his scarred face. His palm, bearing the mark of a jagged scar, hung at his side as he approached the restrained man.

Artemis translated quickly.

"Then why am I tied up?" Enzo growled back to her in Italian, his voice laced with frustration and anger.

"Because we need your cooperation, and given your size and strength, it seemed like the best way to ensure our safety while we talk to you," Artemis replied calmly.

"Listen, Enzo," Artemis said, taking the lead. She leaned against a rickety table that seemed to groan under her weight. "We're not your enemies here. We want the same thing you do—to find Matteo."

Enzo's eyes flickered between Forester and Artemis, the tension palpable in the air. The shack felt like it was closing in on them, the darkness outside pressing against the single window. Outside, the wind whispered through the trees, as if urging them to hurry.

"Enzo, please," Artemis added softly, her eyes imploring him to understand. "We can help each other."

Forester could see the gears turning in Enzo's head, the man's struggle evident on his sweat-soaked face. The side of his head was bleeding from where Forester had struck him.

Artemis's gaze locked on Enzo. "Tell us everything that happened when Matteo disappeared," she demanded, keeping her voice firm but controlled.

"Go to hell!" Enzo spat, his face contorting with rage. He tugged at the ropes binding him to the chair, veins bulging in his biceps and neck as he strained against his restraints. His fury was palpable in the small dimly lit shack.

"Enzo, we're not your enemies," Artemis interjected softly. Her chimeric eyes fixed on him, unwavering, as though trying to pierce through the thick wall of anger he had erected around himself. "We just need to know what you saw or heard."

"You're behind this! I knew it. I told him."

"We're not. We're trying to help. If you help us . . ."

"Ha! And why should I help you?" Enzo snarled, sneering at them both. The air in the room grew heavy, charged with the energy of his defiance.

"Every second we waste is another second Matteo remains in the hands of those who took him," she said evenly. "If you truly want to see him safe, to do your job, you'll help us. If not, then your silence will be just as damning as the actions of those who abducted him."

Enzo's nostrils flared, his chest heaving as he glared at them both. Artemis could see the wheels turning in his mind, weighing the consequences of cooperation against the potential costs of withholding information. After a tense moment, Enzo's shoulders slumped ever so slightly.

"We wouldn't be talking, would we?" she said simply. "Think about it. If we didn't want Matteo safe, why would we be talking to you? Hmm?"

He paused at this and actually seemed swayed by her words. He hesitated briefly, bit his lip, then said, "You really aren't involved?"

"No!"

"Swear it."

"I swear it."

He scowled at her. "If you're lying, I'll hunt you down. I'll tear you to pieces."

"What's he saying?" Forester whispered.

Artemis ignored her partner. Instead, she said, "Understood, Enzo. But I'm not lying."

"Alright," he grunted, defeat lacing his voice. "I'll tell you what I know."

Artemis's gaze bore into Enzo as she felt a flicker of relief. But this case was getting stranger. She could've sworn they'd found the killer. But he was dead back at a vineyard. And he'd died at the same time Matteo had disappeared. "Let's start with the basics. Where were you when Matteo was taken?"

"Right outside his room," Enzo grunted, his massive frame straining against the ropes that held him to the rickety chair.

"But it all happened so fast. One moment he was there, the next . . . gone."

"Did you see anyone? Any suspicious activity?" Artemis probed, her voice cool and calculated.

"Nothing!" Enzo spat, his eyes darting around the room as if seeking an escape from the relentless questioning. "I told you, I didn't see anything!"

"Think harder," Artemis pressed, her piercing gaze never leaving his face. "You must have noticed something—a figure, a sound. Anything could be important."

"Damn it, woman!" Enzo barked, veins popping on his temples. "Do you think I'm holding back on purpose? There was nothing! Nothing!"

Forester watched as Artemis remained unflappable in the face of Enzo's raw fury. She leaned forward slightly, her tone shifting to something more empathetic. "Enzo, we understand how difficult this is for you, but we need your help. We can't find Matteo without the information you hold. Don't let anger cloud your judgment."

Enzo conceded, his knuckles white as he clenched his hands into fists. "There was one thing. A smell. It was faint, but I caught a whiff of it just before Matteo vanished. Like . . . flowers."

"Like perfume?"

"Maybe."

"Good," Artemis said, her voice softening. "That's a start. Anything else you can remember?"

"Maybe . . ." Enzo hesitated, his eyes flicking back and forth between Forester and Artemis as if sizing them up. "There was this sound—a soft whirring. It was there for a split second, then gone."

A bead of sweat trickled down Enzo's temple, tracing the curve of his jaw as it dripped from his chin. He swallowed hard, the muscles in his throat working with the effort as he hesitated. The room seemed to shrink around them, the silence punctuated only by the creaking of the old wooden floorboards beneath their feet.

"Fine," Enzo finally admitted, his voice filled with frustration and guilt. "I wasn't with Matteo when he was taken. I should've been there, but I . . . I wasn't."

The confession weighed heavily on his chest as if a boulder had been placed upon him. Artemis gave him a measured look, her eyes sharp and calculating.

"Enzo, it's crucial that we know every detail, no matter how small or seemingly insignificant," she urged, her voice steady.

"Did you hear a car during the incident? Anything that could help us understand what happened?"

Enzo rubbed his wrists where the ropes had left angry red marks, his face contorting in concentration.

"No," he said at last, shaking his head. "I didn't hear a car. It was eerily quiet—like the world stood still for a moment."

Artemis nodded, her hair drifting across her shoulders as she digested this new information. She glanced at Forester, who mirrored her thoughtful expression. If there had been no car, then how had Matteo disappeared so swiftly and without a trace?

Enzo's admission added another layer of complexity to the mystery that had ensnared them. It was a puzzle they were determined to solve, piece by piece.

Artemis shifted her gaze from Enzo's bound form to the single window in the shack, where a beam of sunlight cast long shadows across the room. Enzo's eyes narrowed as he hesitated, struggling to recall any details of that fateful moment.

"Are you certain, Enzo?" she asked, her tone soft yet insistent. "That there was no car? This is important. We need to know exactly what happened."

Enzo nodded, his expression darkening with resolve. "I'm sure. I didn't hear a car. I would've remembered it, I swear."

Artemis exchanged a glance with Forester, who leaned against the far wall, his arms folded across his chest. They both recognized the importance of this revelation. In the back of her mind, Artemis envisioned the pieces of the puzzle rearranging themselves, coming together to form new patterns and connections.

"Alright," she said slowly, her eyes never leaving Enzo's face. "Thank you for your honesty. This information could be vital in helping us find Matteo."

She glanced at Forester, and he raised an eyebrow as if to say really? She nodded, watching him. She gestured toward the door.

"Wait!" Enzo cried. "You can't leave me!"

"There's a knife under the table," she called back.

Then, as he cursed after them, Artemis and Forester hurried away. They strode side by side.

"What are you thinking?" Forester asked as they moved through the woods behind the subdivision where the mobster had been taken.

"I'm thinking"—Artemis paused, moving quickly through the woods, her feet pressing against fallen leaves, her brow creased in deep thought—"that we're looking for a woman."

"How's that?"

"The perfume," she said simply. "And no car."

"Women . . . don't like cars?"

Artemis shook her head. "Remember what Jon told us? Remember what the caretaker saw?"

"The bike?"

"A left-handed person on a woman's bike. What if the easiest explanation is the real one. What if the bike belonged to a woman . . . and there was no car because she was on that bike again."

"How did she get the old mobster out by bike?"

"A trolley. Something attached. Maybe she hid the bike nearby and led him away on foot at gunpoint."

"So who is this mysterious woman?"

Artemis wrinkled her nose. "Someone who was working with Leo Giroud."

"So you think there's two of them?"

She paused. "Maybe . . . or maybe Leo was the man who found their targets. But the woman? She was the real attack dog."

"Giroud killed a man in the car."

"I know. I saw that. A necessary evil, perhaps?"

Artemis and Forester both went quiet as they proceeded to their parked car.

"So who's this woman?"

"Someone who either wore the same watch as Leo . . . or who was given the same watch as Leo."

"The Rolex?"

"The one on the security footage, yes."

"But who could it be?"

Artemis paused briefly, shaking her head. "I don't know . . . but we need to look into Leo's girlfriends . . . sisters. Anyone close to him."

Forester had his phone out and had been scrolling on it. At Artemis's words, he paused. She noticed this motion as he reached the front door of their car.

"What is it?" she said quickly.

He glanced at her, eyes wide.

"What? You find something?"

He turned his phone to her. "Leo Giroud has a twin sister," Forester said.

Artemis leaned in, gaping. A woman who hadn't been in the video she'd studied with her father, but one clearly apparent in a family photo from a few years ago. A smiling, pretty woman. A woman wearing a matching watch to her brother's.

"Marietta Giroud," Artemis said quietly. She stared at the image, memorizing it.

"Where do you think we'll find her?"

"I don't know, but we need to figure that out. If we don't, Matteo is dead."

"Is that such a bad thing?" Forester muttered.

Artemis ignored this comment. She said, "For Tommy's sake, I can't let that happen. Come on, let's go!"

They both slipped into the car as Artemis pulled her phone out and placed a quick call.

CHAPTER 23

THE CRISP AUTUMN AIR was heavy with tension as Marietta Giroud held Matteo Riccardo at gunpoint, her finger trembling on the trigger. The cold steel of the weapon in her hand felt like both a burden and a necessary means to an end. She stared intently into Riccardo's eyes, searching for any signs of defiance or deception.

"Wheel that bicycle," she commanded, gesturing toward a beaten-up two-wheeler leaning against a nearby tree. "And don't you dare look back."

Riccardo's face twisted in fear and confusion, but he didn't question her. He reached out a shaky hand to grasp the handlebars, his once-confident demeanor now shattered under the weight of his precarious situation.

As they began their slow trek down the narrow trail, Marietta's thoughts raced, a storm of emotions threatening to overwhelm her. Two months ago, when Leo had proposed the idea, she had never imagined herself in this position—taking charge of another person's life, let alone someone like Riccardo. But then again, the case against the four horsemen had fallen through. The police had abandoned it.

Someone had to do something.

"Keep moving," she urged Riccardo, her voice barely above a whisper but laced with a steely determination. She couldn't afford any distractions or second thoughts; not when she had come so far.

The crunching of leaves beneath their feet filled the otherwise silent woods, punctuated only by the creaking wheels of the bicycle.

"Almost there," she murmured to herself, steeling her resolve as they approached their destination. The menacingly knotted trees loomed overhead, leaning out over the trail, but Marietta's grip on the gun never wavered. She knew what she had to do.

The damp earth beneath Marietta's boots squelched with every step, the sound a grotesque reminder of her ultimate goal. Her grip on the gun tightened as she led Riccardo farther along the trail, his hands shaking as he clutched the bicycle.

"Please," Riccardo began, his voice barely a whisper. "I didn't mean for it to go this far."

"Quiet!" Marietta snapped, her hatred for him growing by the second. Images of her true father figure flooded her mind—the protective arm around her shoulders, the steady guidance through life's trials. That man had been everything Riccardo was not, and his absence only fueled her rage.

"Listen to me, Marietta," Riccardo pleaded, desperation seeping into his tone. "We can work something out. You don't have to do this."

"Work something out?" Marietta's voice dripped with contempt. "Like those deals you made behind closed doors to avoid prison? The lives you ruined without a second thought?"

Riccardo's face paled, but he continued. "You know how these things work. It's just business. Nothing personal."

"Nothing personal?" A bitter laugh escaped Marietta's lips.

He knew better than to push the point. Leo and Marietta had lost someone they'd loved, and now Riccardo was going to do the same.

The only person he loved, though, was himself.

A bead of sweat rolled down Riccardo's brow, glistening in the fading sunlight. His eyes darted from side to side, searching for an escape route that would never come.

"Y-you're making a mistake," he stammered, his bravado crumbling. "You think they'll let you get away with this? They'll hunt you down like an animal."

"Then so be it," Marietta replied coldly. She could feel his fear wrapping around her like a vise, tightening its grip with every passing moment. But she refused to falter. This was her chance to right the wrongs of the past.

"Please," Riccardo whispered again, his eyes wide with terror. "I'll do anything."

Marietta could feel the damp grass beneath her boots, slick with dew as she led Riccardo through the misty graveyard. The air hung heavy and silent, pierced only by the old mobster's continued begging.

"Please, Marietta," he implored, his voice hoarse and desperate. "I've made mistakes, I know that, but it doesn't have to end this way."

His once-fancy suit was now stained with mud, as if nature itself were passing judgment on him. She couldn't help but think how fitting it was for a man like Riccardo to meet his end in such a place—surrounded by the cold, unyielding stones of those who had gone before him.

"Silence," she commanded.

Riccardo seemed to sense the resolve within her, but still, he tried one last futile plea. "My family . . . you wouldn't want them to suffer, would you? Have mercy, for their sake."

"Mercy?" Marietta's voice turned icy. "You never showed any mercy."

She forced herself to focus on each step they took, the crunch of gravel underfoot, the cool touch of the fog that curled around the headstones of the graveyard. She willed her racing heart to slow, her breaths to come steady and even. Every detail of the scene etched itself into her memory.

"Stop here," she said at last, her voice steady as they reached a small clearing in the graveyard. The moonlight filtered through the dense fog, arriving as if it were a witness to the mobster's execution.

"Please," Riccardo whispered one final time, his bravado long gone, replaced by pure terror.

Marietta stared at him, her face impassive but her mind a storm of conflicting emotions—anger and grief, pain and satisfaction all vying for dominance.

"Dig," she ordered, her voice cold and unyielding.

Marietta glanced at the gnarled tree nearby, its twisted limbs reaching out like skeletal fingers in the darkness. A shovel leaned against the rough bark, its blade glinting ominously in the dim light. She gestured toward it, her tone unyielding. "There's your tool. Use it."

Riccardo hesitated for a moment before shuffling toward the shovel. He reached out a trembling hand, his gaze darting between the implement and Marietta's unwavering stare. As his fingers closed around the handle, he dropped to his knees, overcome by the gravity of his situation.

"Please, don't do this," he begged, tears streaming down his hollow cheeks. "I'll give you anything you want. Money, power, whatever you desire."

"Your money means nothing to me," she replied coldly. "And as for power, I already have that. In this moment, I hold your life in my hands."

Riccardo's eyes widened with terror as he stared up at her, searching for any hint of mercy or compassion—but finding none. He lowered his gaze to the shovel, tears mingling with sweat on his pallid skin.

"Please," he whispered, defeated.

"Dig," Marietta ordered, her voice devoid of emotion. A pregnant moment passed, then she watched as Riccardo began to dig his own grave, each shovelful of earth an act of penance for the lives he had destroyed.

Marietta's eyes narrowed, her grip on the gun tightening. The cold steel pressed against her palm, a chilling reminder of her purpose in this fog-shrouded graveyard. She could see the sweat beading on Riccardo's forehead, his face a mask of terror as he clung to the handle of the shovel.

"Please," he whispered hoarsely, desperation evident in every syllable. "There must be another way."

"No," she said simply. "There is no other way."

With a resigned sigh, Riccardo leaned forward, pressing the blade of the shovel into the soft soil. Each shovelful of dirt felt like a weight lifted from Marietta's heart. This act would never erase the pain Riccardo had caused, but it was a start—a necessary step toward justice.

"Quicker," she urged, watching as Riccardo's pace increased, sweat pouring down his face in rivulets.

She glanced over her shoulder. The coming evening brought a strange silence, and the silence made her uneasy. Where was the noise? Where was Leo?

He often came before the end . . . So where was her brother?

She frowned and turned back to find the old mobster watching her. Her voice cracked like a whip. "I said dig!"

And so he dug.

CHAPTER 24

THE FOG HUNG LIKE a shroud over the forest, tendrils of mist creeping between gnarled branches and twining around the trunks of ancient trees. Artemis's skin was slick with the moisture, her breaths coming in puffs as she jogged alongside Forester. There was an unsettling quietness to the woods, as though they were holding their breath, waiting for some unknown danger to reveal itself. The air was heavy with tension, making the hairs on the back of her neck stand on end.

Forester's long strides barely made a sound on the damp earth, his disheveled hair plastered to his forehead by the fog. His scarred face remained stoic, but the intensity of the situation was evident in his dark eyes as they navigated the treacherous terrain.

Artemis kept glancing toward the device clutched in Forester's hand. The phone was facing up, and the screen glowed brightly.

"Left?" Forester confirmed.

A long sigh crackled through the speaker. "I already told you," snapped the irritated voice of Agent Desmond Wade.

Artemis had been in the car when Cameron had placed the second call to his ex-partner. The FBI agent had been none too happy about receiving another call.

"Forester," came the curt reply from Agent Wade, his annoyance at being contacted again evident in his tone. "I'm not your damn GPS. You said it would just take a minute."

Forester was breathing heavily from the trek, but he slowed his jog now.

"Listen, Wade, this isn't a social call. We're in trouble," Forester insisted, his voice edged with desperation.

"Look, Forester," Wade snapped, his impatience clearly audible, even through the tinny speaker, "I told you last time that I wasn't going to do any more favors for you and Artemis. You two are on your own."

Artemis could see the muscles in Forester's jaw tighten as he clenched his teeth, a testament to the frustration he was trying to keep contained. She knew they were asking a lot of Wade, but there was no one else they could turn to in this situation. And time was running out. They no longer had the federal resources to track phones, and they needed to find Marietta Giroud.

"Desmond," Forester began, his voice steady and persuasive, "I know we've asked much of you in the past, and I understand your reluctance. But we wouldn't be contacting you now if it weren't absolutely necessary. There's a life at stake here."

There was a pause on the other end of the line, and Artemis held her breath, knowing that the next words spoken would either make or break their mission. The silence stretched on, thick with tension, until it seemed almost suffocating.

"A life . . ." Forester wheedled. "Wasn't that always what you were telling me? To care about others? Hmm? Look at me. I'm a big boy now. All the care."

"Shut up, Cameron."

"So is that a yes?"

"I already told you 'go left', didn't I?" Wade finally sighed, his annoyance palpable. "But this is the last time, Forester. After this, you're on your own."

"Thank you, Wade," Forester replied, genuine gratitude coloring his words. "We owe you one."

Artemis couldn't help but feel a mixture of relief and apprehension wash over her. They had managed to secure the assistance they desperately needed, but at what cost? Would this be the last straw for Agent Wade?

Forester glanced at her, his scarred face betraying none of the anxiety she was sure must be churning inside him. "Let's move," he said tersely, and they resumed their frantic pace through the woods.

In the back of her mind, Artemis knew that they couldn't keep relying on others to bail them out of dangerous situations. But for now, it was all they had. And she couldn't help but be grateful for Forester's ability to win people over, even when the odds were stacked against them.

"Where is she?" Artemis interjected, trying to keep her own voice steady despite the rapid pounding of her heart.

"Northwest of your current position, but the signal's weak. You need to hurry." Wade's voice was clipped but professional.

Artemis and Forester exchanged a glance, their eyes communicating volumes in that split second. There was no time to waste. They sprang into action, tearing through the damp undergrowth, following Agent Wade's terse directions as they raced against the clock.

"Take a left at the next fork," Wade instructed, his impatience evident in every syllable.

As they sprinted, Artemis felt the moisture from the leaves seep through her clothes, chilling her skin. She couldn't let herself be distracted by discomfort; a life was on the line. Forester's scarred hand gripped his phone tightly, sweat beading on his brow as they plunged deeper into the misty woods.

"Are we getting closer?" Forester panted into the phone, his breath ragged from exertion.

"Maybe," Wade replied. "The signal's fluctuating. I can't pin her down exactly."

Artemis gritted her teeth, cursing the limitations of technology. What if they were too late? What if they couldn't find Marietta in time? She forced herself to focus, pushing her tired legs forward, following Forester's lead as they navigated the treacherous terrain.

"Right there!" Wade barked suddenly. "Due north of your position!"

"Got it," Forester acknowledged, his voice strained as they veered off the path and into the thick undergrowth.

Artemis could feel the adrenaline coursing through her veins, sharpening her senses and propelling her onward.

"Almost there." Wade urged them on, his impatience now tinged with a hint of concern.

Artemis scarcely had time to process his words before her foot caught on a hidden root, sending her sprawling to the ground. Pain seared through her ankle as she let out a cry of frustration.

"Artemis!" Forester called, skidding to a halt beside her. His eyes were wide with worry, but she waved him off.

Gritting her teeth, Artemis forced herself to stand, placing weight on her injured ankle. She ignored the jolt of pain that shot up her leg and shifted her focus to the task at hand.

Forester waited, a hand outstretched in case she needed the aid. But she gingerly tested her foot, then gave a quick shake of her head. "I'm alright," she whispered. "Just fine."

Forester frowned.

Artemis's ears pricked at the distant echo of a gunshot, a chilling sound that sliced through the fog-shrouded graveyard. Her heart slammed into her ribs as she skidded to a halt, eyes darting in search of Forester. The pounding of her feet against the damp ground had been replaced by a sudden silence that hung heavily in the air.

"Forester," she whispered urgently. "Did you hear that?"

"Yeah . . . means we're getting close."

Their synchronization, honed over countless hours spent working together, was evident in their matching strides and the unspoken understanding that passed between them. As they navigated the labyrinth of tombstones, Artemis felt a flicker of gratitude for their partnership—she couldn't imagine facing this unfolding enigma without Forester by her side.

"Could Marietta have fired that shot?" she asked, unable to keep the tremor from her voice.

"Uncertain," Forester replied, his brow furrowed with concern. "But we can't rule it out."

A cold shiver crept up Artemis's spine, a sensation she instinctively knew wasn't caused by the dampness clinging to her skin. She shook off the dark thoughts that threatened to consume her and focused on the task at hand.

As they ventured deeper into the gloom, every muscle in Artemis's body tensed, each nerve strung taut like a bowstring.

Then, Wade's voice crackled. "She's up ahead. Graveyard. Now, I'm leaving." He hung up. Forester stared at the phone, frowning.

But then, Artemis pointed through the mist. "I see it," she whispered.

The tombstones arose from the ground like teeth, jutting amid the mist. She stared into the dark, her heart pounding in her chest. No more gunshots. No more sounds at all except for her labored breathing.

Forester and Artemis cautiously approached the graveyard, both moving silently, feet stilled and muffled by the leaves underfoot. Artemis's eyes scanned the surroundings, searching for any sign of Marietta. There was no movement, no indication of life among the tombstones. The silence was oppressive, broken only by the sound of their own breathing.

"Stay alert," Forester murmured, his hand hovering near his hip where his gun was holstered. "We don't know what we're walking into."

Artemis nodded, her senses on high alert as they crept forward. She could feel her heart pounding in her chest, each beat feeling like a cannon shot in the stillness of the graveyard.

They moved in tandem, their footsteps measured and cautious as they weaved between the graves. Artemis's eyes roved over the headstones, searching for any sign of Marietta or their assailants. She saw nothing but the fog and the damp earth beneath her feet.

"Over here," Forester whispered, his voice stark in the stillness. He was crouched behind a particularly large headstone, his hand gesturing for her to join him.

Artemis crept forward, her eyes scanning the area around the grave. She saw no one, but the hairs on the back of her neck prickled with a sense of unease.

"What is it?" she asked, her voice barely above a whisper.

Forester didn't answer, his eyes fixed on a small bundle of fabric on the ground beside the grave. Artemis's eyes followed his gaze, and she saw what he was looking at—a tattered backpack, mud-streaked and frayed around the edges.

"Someone's definitely here."

"That was a gunshot earlier, wasn't it?" Artemis whispered.

Forester nodded.

"So where is she?"

Forester shook his head, the two of them standing alone in the dark, both of them tense. And then they heard a faint groaning sound.

"Forester. . ." Artemis said.

"I heard it," he replied, tense.

The sound grew louder. Artemis looked around, but there was no discernible source of the noise. The groaning increased, but it was faint, muffled, as if distant and yet so close . . .

She looked one way, then the other . . .

And then she spotted the muddy shovel leaning against the tree. She stared at it. The blade was covered in wet, fresh mud. Blood streaked the handle. She blinked, then looked at the ground. Freshly turned earth. Packed earth.

"Forester . . ."

This time he followed her gaze.

"Forester, I think he's buried."

Forester's eyes widened as he took in the sight before them. The muddy shovel, the fresh earth . . . It was all too clear what had happened here.

"Artemis, we have to dig him out," Forester said, his voice urgent.

Artemis nodded, heart pounding in her chest. They surged forward at the same time. Artemis moved forward, falling on hands and knees to scoop the fresh earth with her hands. Forester surged forward, snatched the shovel, and raised the point to dig.

"Stop!" Artemis cried. "You'll kill him! He's not deep. I see fingers."

Indeed, there, in the earth, horribly, she spotted a curled hand with fingers barely visible. She leaned closer, her heart in her throat, as Forester dropped beside her to dig with his palms. The groaning grew louder, more insistent, as they worked frantically to free the buried man.

Finally, Forester's hand came away holding the lapel of a jacket. He clawed the wet ground like a wild dog. Artemis helped as well, her fingers scooping through the mud, frantically digging as she breathed in panting huffs.

And that's when she spotted the shadowy figure. Watching—staring at them. A thin, frail thing, a black hood upraised. Left-handed, just like her twin brother.

Marietta Giroud stood a few dozen paces away, as still as the trees around her.

She stared at where they dug, and the moment she realized she'd been spotted, she cursed and turned on her heel to run.

"Hey!" Artemis shouted. "Hey, stop!"

But Marietta was sprinting away.

Forester continued to dig at the ground, and a few seconds later, a face emerged. "He's not breathing!"

Artemis turned back, frantic.

"Go!" Forester was yelling at her. "Go, I've got this!"

Forester had only half dragged the old mobster from the muddy hole.

At the same time, Artemis gave him a quick look as if to say, *Are you sure?* When she received a nod, she burst into motion, sprinting after the killer.

Marietta led Artemis through the tombstones, weaving through the mist over the graveyard. Artemis's heart raced as she ran, her eyes trained on Marietta's figure as she disappeared into the fog. She could hear the killer's footsteps pounding against the damp earth, her breaths coming in ragged gasps as she struggled to keep pace.

Marietta was fast, but Artemis was faster. She pushed herself harder, her legs pumping as she closed in on her prey.

Suddenly, Marietta veered to the left, disappearing behind a large headstone. Artemis followed suit, her heart pounding in her chest as she approached the grave. She rounded the headstone, her gun drawn and ready, but Marietta was nowhere to be seen. Her breaths came in short gasps, her heart pounding in her chest as she scanned the area for any sign of the killer.

And then, she heard a sound behind her. She spun around, gun raised, and found herself face-to-face with Marietta.

Marietta's eyes were wild, her face contorted with rage as she aimed her gun at Artemis. "You shouldn't have followed me," she snarled.

Artemis didn't flinch, her own gun steady in her hand. "You shouldn't have buried him," she replied calmly.

Marietta's eyes flickered with fear for a moment, but then she regained her composure. "He was an old monster; he was going to die anyway," she spat. "I put him out of his misery."

Artemis shook her head. "You don't get to decide who lives and who dies," she said firmly. "Put down your weapon."

The two women held their guns pointed at one another.

Marietta's hand was shaking, her eyes darting around the grave-yard as she tried to find an escape. But Artemis could see the fear in Marietta's eyes, the desperation as she searched for a way out.

"Put the gun down," Artemis repeated. "I don't want to hurt you."

Marietta's eyes narrowed in anger, her finger tightening on the trigger. "You're just like them," she hissed. "You don't understand anything."

Artemis didn't respond, her finger lightly tensing, ready on the trigger. She knew that Marietta was dangerous, that she would do anything to get away. But she also knew that she couldn't let her go, not after what she had done.

"The only way you live is if I turn you over to the police," Artemis said quietly.

Marietta scowled at her. "Is that a threat? Where are you from? Your accent is heavy."

Artemis didn't reply to this dig at her Italian. She'd been practicing, and like her sister, Artemis's ability to pick up languages on the fly was directly related to her capacity for memory.

She kept her weapon steady.

Briefly, as she noticed the way she clutched her gun, Artemis realized how much had changed in her life.

She remembered a time when the sight of a weapon had triggered a panic attack. But now? Now . . . she held the gun, unwavering, her eyes narrowed as she stared at the figure in front of her.

Things had changed, but one thing remained the same. She couldn't hand this woman over to the mobsters. But she also couldn't let her get away.

"I'm going to give your name to the authorities," Artemis said quietly, "and the mob will find out. They want you dead."

"You work for them."

"No, I don't."

"Liar!"

"I'm not."

Artemis spoke quietly, firmly. She continued, "If you want to live, you're going to turn yourself in. It's that simple."

Marietta was slowly backing away, but with each step she took back, Artemis took one forward. The leaves crunched underfoot.

Behind Marietta, a stagnant, pale pond spread out. It might have been beautiful once, but now the ghostly water had a haunted wildness to it as Marietta's foot touched the water, spreading ripples through the murky surface.

"Put it down!" Artemis said even more fiercely.

"You don't know what they did," she replied just as firmly. "All of them. They deserved to die."

"You don't get to make that call."

"I do! I did," she snapped.

She was beautiful, but her features were gaunt now, strained. Sweat slicked her face, and the rage in her eyes marred her otherwise attractive features.

"He killed him . . ."

The *he* and the *him* didn't require interpretation.

"They all did," she continued. "They had blood on their hands. For years! No one did anything. No one!"

Artemis didn't speak, just allowing the woman to express her fury.

Marietta's hand was still shaking, but she didn't lower her gun. "You don't know what it's like," she said, her voice trembling with emotion. "To watch someone you love suffer at the hands of those monsters. To know that they'll never face justice. I had to do something."

Artemis could see the pain in Marietta's eyes, the raw emotion that had driven her to take the law into her own hands. She knew that the woman was dangerous, but she also knew that she was desperate.

"You can't keep running," Artemis said softly. "It's over. Turn yourself in."

Marietta didn't respond, her eyes fixed on Artemis's face. For a moment, there was silence. She looked as if she might even be considering the option, as if she'd tired herself out by her raging.

But then Artemis said, "Don't end up like Leo. Don't end up like your twin."

She froze and stared at Artemis. "What happened to Leo?"

Artemis stared back. "I . . . what?"

"What . . . happened . . . to my brother?" she said, her voice low, dangerous.

Artemis realized in her exhaustion she'd made a horrible miscalculation. The woman didn't know her brother was dead. Didn't know Leo had shot himself. Now, Artemis just froze, at a complete loss for words, which was a rarity for her.

She opened her mouth, then closed it again, and Marietta's eyes widened.

"No . . ." she whispered, reading Artemis's silence. "No . . . you're lying . . ."

Artemis winced. "I'm . . . I'm so sorry."

Marietta screamed, raising her gun.

Artemis lunged in, low. She tackled the woman around the waist, bringing her crashing into the small, moonlit pond behind her. The gun went flying, and the two women fell into the water with a loud splash!

CHAPTER 25

THEY THRASHED AND FOUGHT in the water, Artemis trying to keep Marietta restrained while she tried to break free and get to her gun.

The water was murky and dark, bits of algae sticking to their skin as they fought. The sounds of their grunts were muted and muddy in the oppressive underwater world as they fought a desperate battle for control.

Marietta's eyes were wild with rage as she tried to break free from Artemis's grip. She clawed at her face with sharp nails but couldn't seem to gain any ground against the woman holding her back.

Artemis was tireless, determined not to let Marietta escape or harm anyone else ever again. She held on tight despite the woman's struggles, refusing to let go even when Marietta managed a few hits that briefly weakened her grip.

Marietta continued to scramble back, deeper and deeper into the turbid water. But Artemis refused to let go. Now, her feet no longer touched the silty floor. Water was in Artemis's mouth, tasting stale. Her lips were cold, and her clothing soaked, her hair plastered to her face, trailing droplets as her bangs whipped around.

Marietta feinted forward once, twice, and then the second time managed to avoid Artemis's grasp. She wrapped her fingers around Artemis's neck, giving her throat a claw-like squeeze. Artemis's fingers scrambled against the woman's wrist.

Artemis felt the panic rising in her chest as she struggled to breathe. Her vision blurred as the world around her began to fade. Her grip on Marietta loosened as her body weakened.

But just as Artemis was about to lose consciousness, she saw a glint of metal in the water. Her fingers brushed against it, and she realized it was Marietta's gun, fallen into the pond during their struggle.

Summoning the last of her strength, Artemis reached for the gun and grasped it tightly. She brought the barrel up to Marietta's neck, but she couldn't bring herself to point the barrel at the woman. So instead she raised it higher, near the woman's ear.

And as Artemis choked, she fired two shots next to the side of the woman's face, near her ear. The gun pointed skyward, but the sound reverberated, startling Marietta.

Marietta's grip on Artemis's throat loosened as she yelped in surprise, the gunshots resounding in the air. Struggling backward, still floundering in the water, Marietta clapped a hand to her ear as if she were putting pressure on a wound.

Artemis now had the gun. She was exhausted, though, and Marietta wasn't going anywhere. So instead of chasing the woman further out into the water, Artemis kicked in the murk and headed back to the shore.

She gasped for air as she made for the shore, coughing and sputtering. Artemis dragged herself out of the pond and collapsed on the ground, her body shaking with exhaustion and adrenaline.

As the pounding in her ears subsided, the silence of the forest was now broken by the sound of sirens in the distance. Artemis knew she had to get out of there before the police arrived. She got up slowly, her limbs still shaking, and pointed the gun toward where Marietta was still treading water.

She was shaking, trembling, gasping. She no longer looked like a killer in control. But rather, she just looked small and sad. She stared at where Artemis pointed her gun, shaking like a leaf. Artemis could now see the woman was openly weeping.

"Do it," she whispered.

Artemis didn't reply.

"DO IT!" Marietta demanded. "Kill me, please." Her voice carried a deep, painful moan.

And as she tread water, trying to drag herself further out into the pond, away from the shore, Artemis felt a flicker of sympathy.

This woman . . . this woman in pain had lost her brother. Artemis knew what that was like. This woman in pain had killed three men and attempted to kill another . . . Artemis couldn't play God. Couldn't decide on a reprieve . . .

But she couldn't turn Marietta over to the authorities either. At least . . . not this way.

"You can still live," Artemis said simply. "Think of your uncle. Your father," she said quickly. "Do it for them. The living and the dead."

Marietta was still shaking.

"I know it feels like the world is falling apart, but it doesn't have to."

"I'll spend the rest of my life in prison," she whispered, her voice coming in gasps from the effort it took to keep her swimming.

Artemis shook her head. "Not if you cut a deal. You know a lot about the mob. About these men you targeted. You can tell them everything you know. Cut a deal with the authorities. They'll play ball. They want these guys as much as you do. Not just the men you killed but their subordinates. The rest of the organization."

Marietta didn't look as if she could really even hear what Artemis was saying. Artemis felt her heart go out to the woman, but she said, more insistently, "There's no point, Marietta. No point in fighting any longer."

"What are you going to do?"

Artemis hesitated. "I'll give the mob their boss back. Alive. That'll be enough."

"Enough for what?" Marietta whispered.

But Artemis ignored this question. "Come to shore," Artemis insisted. "Please."

Marietta stared. "Leo's dead . . ."

"You're alive. Make a difference with your political inroads. Do something with your life. Make a deal; do something good. Change things." Artemis knew she was grasping at straws now.

Marietta looked exhausted. She looked ready to drift away.

Artemis murmured, "Your father is past their ability to hurt him. Think of your uncle. He's already lost his nephew today. Is he going to lose you too?"

Marietta let out a strangled sob. Then, reluctantly, with weak, frail movements, she began to pull herself to shore. Artemis felt a flicker of exhaustion, and she lowered the gun as the killer scrambled from the murk, collapsed on the muddy ground, and wept.

CHAPTER 26

ARTEMIS AND FORESTER SAT side by side in the small airplane they'd chartered. Fake names, fake passports. They were on the move again.

Tommy was in the back of the plane, sleeping. No longer on a hit list. Their bank account was two million lighter . . .

"She really did it, huh?" Forester whispered, his eyes half-hooded from where he'd been dozing off.

Artemis glanced at the man. "What?"

"Marietta went full witness protection program."

Artemis sighed and nodded. She didn't know if what she'd done was right. She didn't much want to think about it either way. "Think we'll be safe this time?" Artemis whispered.

"I hope so," Forester said.

Artemis glanced next to Tommy where Helen was sleeping. Otto was up front, trying to give their pilot some pointers.

Some things never changed.

Artemis let out a weary and exhausted sigh. She leaned her head against Forester's shoulder. "Where are we going?"

"To paradise," Cameron murmured.

She shifted a bit, trying to find a more comfortable position, her cheek resting on his warm arm. "Oh?"

"Yes . . ." he trailed off, and there was something strained in his voice.

"What is it?" she said.

He looked at her. "Nothing . . . Nothing . . ."

She frowned now, sitting up. She stared him in the eyes. "Where are we going, Cameron?"

He sighed. "Tropical island. I have history there. I know the locals. We'll be safe."

"You're sure?"

"Positive. The governor owes me his life."

Artemis blinked in surprise. "R-really?"

He nodded.

Then, her mind connected the dots. "Wait . . . an island? Isn't that where . . ." She swallowed.

"Where she died, yes."

"Your wife?"

"I wouldn't go back with anyone else. But I'll go with you."

He said it with such certainty that she felt a lump form in her throat. "Are you sure?"

"We'll be safe. And . . ."

"And what?"

"Something with that soldier wasn't right."

"The man who killed your wife?"

"I don't think he did it alone."

"What?"

She sat upright now, staring at Cameron.

"Something he said . . . He was a mercenary. A gun for hire. He enjoyed his killing . . . but he was a weapon."

"So?"

"So I messed him up. Pretty damn good. And he came after me. But whoever put him on to me . . . That's who I want."

"And you think we'll find the person who hired the killer on the island?"

Forester leaned back, crossing his arms, his face troubled. "I think so. But mostly, we'll be safe. Just trust me, Artemis. You do trust me, don't you?" He glanced at her.

She smiled and realized, with very little doubt, she absolutely did. She nodded once. She felt equal parts sad and tired. Sad for Forester. Sad for all the death.

But contented too. Something about flying twenty-thousand feet above the sea, whipping through the air, without any troubles in the world except the desire to remain aloft . . .

It felt . . . right somehow.

She nodded and snuggled against her boyfriend. As she drifted off to sleep, she murmured, "Any leads on who might've hired the hit man?"

Cameron swallowed, hesitated, then said, "I think it was my brother."

Artemis looked up again, staring. "I didn't know you had a brother." Her mind floundered for a moment as her unease at the accusation mingled with her simple desire to know more about the man she leaned against. "What is he like?"

"Just like me," Cameron said quietly. "But he plays for the other team."

"What, like a criminal?"

"Mhmm."

Artemis frowned, troubled. Cameron had a brother? A friendship with the governor of a paradise island? And he thought his own brother had hired the hit on his wife? She shivered at the thought of it all. But she was also exhausted. Slowly, she put the questions aside, closing her eyes once more.

But she couldn't quite clear her mind; the troubling thoughts lurked, lingering in the darkness of her drowsy brain like wraiths.

The End.

WHAT IS NEXT FOR ARTEMIS BLYTHE?

Are they chasing a murderer or a ghost?

Artemis returns to the paradise island where Forester's wife died in search of answers.

Who really killed her?

And the mystery unleashes a shocking secret that shakes her to the bones. In the end, Artemis Blythe finds herself chasing a decade-old ghost who doesn't seem bound by the normal laws of physics. Locked doors, stone walls, gravity--the killer seems to elude even the feters of the physical world to reach his victims.

Her genius has caught killers before, but how does one outwit a murderous opponent who defies the laws of logic?

ALSO BY GEORGIA WAGNER

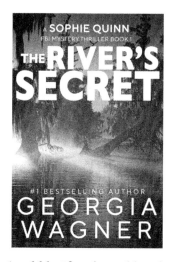

A cold knife, a brutal laugh.

Then the odds-defying escape.

Once a hypnotist with her own TV show, now, Sophie Quinn works as a full-time consultant for the FBI. Everything changed six years ago. She can still remember that horrible night. Slated to be the River Killer's tenth victim, she managed to slip her bindings and barely escape where so many others failed. Her sister wasn't so lucky.

And now the killer is back.

Two PHDs later, she's now a rising star at the FBI. Her photographic memory helps solve crimes, but also helps her to never forget. She saw the River Killer's tattoo. She knows what he sounds like. And now, ten years later, he's active again.

Sophie Quinn heads back home to the swamps of Louisiana, along the Mississippi River, intent on evening the score and finding the man who killed her sister. It's been six years since she's been home, though. Broken relationships and shattered dreams exist among the bayous, the rivers, the waterways and swamps of Louisiana; can Sophie find her way home again? Or will she be the River Killer's next victim to float downstream?

ALSO BY GEORGIA WAGNER

**Once a rising star in the FBI, with the best case closure
rate of any investigator, Ella Porter is now exiled to a small
gold mining town bordering the wilderness of Alaska.
The reason for her new assignment? She allowed a prolific
serial killer to escape custody.**

But what no one knows is that she did it on purpose.

The day she shows up in Nome, bags still unpacked, the wife of the richest gold miner in town goes missing. This is the second woman to vanish in as many days. And it's up to Ella to find out what happened.

Assigning Ella to Nome is no accident, either. Though she swore she'd never return, Ella grew up in the small, gold mining town, treated like royalty as a child due to her own family's wealth. But like all gold tycoons, the Porter family secrets are as dark as Ella's own.

FREE BOOKS AND MORE

Want to see what else the Greenfield authors have written? Go to the website.

Home - Greenfield Press

Or sign up to our newsletter where you will get sneak peaks, exclusive giveaways, behind the scenes content, and more. Plus, you'll be notified of Fan Pricing events when they occur and get exclusive offers from other authors.

Click the link or copy it carefully into your web browser.

Newsletter - Greenfield Press

Prefer social media? Join our thriving Facebook community. Want to join the inner circle where you can keep up to date with everything? This is a free page on Facebook where you can hang out with likeminded individuals and enjoy discussing my books.

There is cake too (but only if you bring it).

Facebook

ABOUT THE AUTHOR

GEORGIA WAGNER WORKED AS a ghost writer for many, many years before finally taking the plunge into self-publishing. Location and character are two big factors for Georgia, and getting those right allows the story to flow seamlessly onto the page. And flow it does, because Georgia is so prolific a new term is required to describe the rate at which nerve-tingling stories find their way into print.

When not found attached to a laptop, Georgia likes spending time in local arboretums, among the trees and ponds. An avid cultivator of orchids, begonias, and all things floral, Georgia also has a strong penchant for art, paintings, and sculptures. A many-decades long passion for mystery novels and years of chess tournament experience makes Georgia the perfect person to pen the Artemis Blythe series.

Printed in Great Britain
by Amazon